The Woman Who Destroyed Christmas

by
M J Hardy

Contents

HAVE YOU READ:

IF TRUE AND UNCONDITIONAL LOVE EXISTS IN THIS WORLD, THEN IT HAS TO BE THE LOVE BETWEEN A MOTHER AND A CHILD.

Urvashi Rautela

THE WOMAN WHO DESTROYED CHRISTMAS

How far would you go to protect your daughter?
When Alice Adams met her daughter's boyfriend, she was far from impressed. He was everything she didn't want for her little girl and so decided to give fate a helping hand.
Luckily, they were invited to spend Christmas with his family which was just the opportunity she needed. Three days to ruin their relationship and save her daughter from a lifetime of regrets.
However, Alice has secrets she hopes her daughter will never discover. In interfering with fate, she unlocks the past with devastating consequences.
As the snow falls and the sleigh bells ring, this will be one Christmas they will all want to forget. There are more than presents under this Christmas tree and as they unwrap the past, the future will never be the same again.
Alice Adams thought she was prepared this Christmas – she was wrong.

PROLOGUE

Standing by my husband's grave watching his coffin lowered into the ground is the best feeling in the world.

My eyes are disguised by dark glasses and I wear black to mourn the fact that I married him in the first place.

The rain beats down on the few people who bothered to come and I shiver a little. Even the heavens weep that such a man was ever born and as I stare at the empty void his carcass now fills, I pity the part of nature that will have to deal with his decomposition.

The priest says a few chosen words and commits his body to the ground. 'Ashes to ashes, dust to dust,' words that are music to my ears.

I stand straight-backed and emotionless as the priest nods for me to approach the grave. He steps back to give me space and I kneel and grasp a handful of earth that sticks to my fingers with the tears of Heaven. It's befitting he is lowered underground because that is sure to be where he is now. In Hell. Sent there by his own choices in life and the actions of a sinner.

Standing straight, I peer into the void and imagine him chained to Satan himself. I relish the sounds of his torture as his soul burns in hell for eternity.

I roll the earth around my fingers and resist the urge to spit on his coffin instead. No, this charade will have to go on for a few moments longer because, after all, I'm good at it.

As I offer a silent prayer of thanks that he was taken, I allow the dirt in my hand to join the one beneath my feet.

My heart sings as I watch it hit the wooden casket with a thud and picture his bitter, twisted face staring up at me in the reality of his death.

A small hand slips into mine and a tiny voice says with a quiver, "Mummy, I'm cold."

Bending down, I pull her coat a little tighter around her shoulders and smile. "Don't worry, darling. Mummy will look after you. Nothing will ever harm you all the time I'm here."

I see the confused face staring up at me as she bites her bottom lip. She takes a look into the giant void and frowns. "Is that daddy?"

I hear the sobs around me as the mourners watch the devastating scene and I shake my head. "No, darling. Daddy is in Heaven with the Angels like I told you. The coffin just holds his body because he no longer has any need for it."

She smiles sweetly and my heart constricts with the purest love. Yes, I would do anything for my daughter - even lie because she is the most important person in the world to me and I will never let anyone hurt her all the time I live.

1

LILY

"I think she liked you."

"Are you sure?"

"Of course, I'm sure. She is my mother, after all."

"I think she's still watching us."

Grinning, I turn around and wave at my mother as she peers through the window. Laughing, I blow her a kiss and take Oliver's hand in mine. "Thanks for that."

"What?"

"Sitting through twenty questions. You did well though."

"Do you think?" He groans and flicks the lock on the car before opening the passenger door like the true gentleman he is.

It doesn't take long before we leave the little street that I call home and head towards the dual carriageway. Oliver, turns on the stereo and the car fills with the latest tracks on Spotify and he breathes a huge sigh of relief. "Well, at least that's out of the way. I was a little nervous, but she seems nice."

"She is, the best actually."

I can tell that Oliver wants to say something but probably doesn't want to hurt my feelings and I know just what it is. My mother is one of the nicest people you would ever want to meet but even I know she is a little over the top sometimes. Maybe it's because I'm all she's got; she's always been a little overprotective. Not that it should concern me but sometimes it's a little stifling.

I know Oliver got a grilling back there. I did pre-warn him but it was worse than usual. That bothers me a little because it's important that my mother likes him.

Looking at him with a sideways glance, my heart beats a little faster as it always does around him and I congratulate myself on finding him in the first place. Oliver Buckland is one of a kind; popular, good looking, funny and thoughtful. Everyone knows Oliver at Uni because he's their star football player and number one on every girl's 'to do' list. Now he's mine and I still can't believe my luck.

"Are you sure she liked me?"

I hear the worry in his voice which makes me smile. For someone who has it all, he is still a little insecure which makes him even more attractive. Reaching across, I grasp his hand and give it a squeeze. "She loved you, Oliver. The fact she asked you so many questions means she could tell I was serious about you. I don't make a habit of taking guys home to meet my mum, you should be honoured."

"I am, it's been a long time coming and I'm glad we finally did it. You know, as far as I'm concerned that was the biggest hurdle we had to face. Now she knows, we can breathe a sigh of relief and start living a normal life with no secrets."

His words remind me why I kept quiet about him for so long. What we didn't tell my mum was that we have been dating seriously for six months already. I never once told her I had fallen completely in love with the most sought-after student on campus and I suppose it was because I couldn't believe he would stay with me. But he did and now with our finals just a few months away, we have the rest of our lives to plan out – together. Yes, my mother had to meet Oliver because ultimately, he will be part of our family one day and not coming from a large one myself, I want that more than anything.

By the time we reach campus, I feel tired. It's been a long day, and the evening spent with my mother was draining. As we park outside the halls of residence he reaches over and drags my lips to his.

Making out in the car with Oliver is every girl's dream. I know the blinds will be twitching as the other students look out and see his unmistakable car. Oliver comes from money and drives the biggest Range Rover any student has ever had. He really does have everything and so do I – him.

Groaning against my lips, he says huskily, "Come back with me tonight. I hate leaving you here."

Laughing, I push him back a little and say firmly. "Not tonight, you know I have that essay that's due in first thing. If I'm going to pass these exams, then I need to step up a gear. I'll see you tomorrow though, breakfast in the Pitstop, usual place?"

He grins and as my heart melts I feel my resolve weakening. I would love to spend every minute of every day and night with him but Mrs Ellwood my economics lecturer is so scary it acts as a good deterrent.

After one more long, lingering kiss, I reluctantly leave the car and head to my dorm and a night spent with google and my economics essay.

My roomie is already in bed and appears to be watching Netflix on her iPad with a million crisp packets littering the bed. She looks up in surprise as I push the door open.

"Hey, Lily, I didn't expect you back tonight, is everything ok?"

I don't miss the hope in her eyes because like everyone else, Nancy idolises Oliver and they are all waiting in the wings for our relationship to end. Feeling a little smug, I shake my head. "Yes, it's all good but unfortunately I have an essay to finish by the morning. I'll be at it all night, so if you like, I'll head to the library so I don't disturb you."

Shaking her head, she casts her iPad aside and sits up looking interested. "So, how did it go? Come on, what did your mother think of Oliver?"

I sit on her bed and grin. "I think she liked him, well, how could she not? He was polite, attentive and answered her questions with good grace and humour. I don't think he put a foot wrong."

"Great, so what next?"

Shrugging, I pick up my folder and iPad. "My essay."

"Not that you idiot. I mean, obviously we break up next week for Christmas, will you get to see darling Oliver over the festive period, or will you have to endure Christmas apart?"

She grins because everyone knows we are inseparable and once again, I feel a little smug as I say, "Actually, Oliver's parents have invited us to spend Christmas with them. We arrive on Christmas Eve and leave on Boxing day. They thought it would be good to meet my mother, and she was surprisingly quite excited about it."

"Man, you lucky…"

I hold up my hand. "I know - you don't have to say it."

As I gather my things, I think back to the look in my mother's eye when Oliver extended his mother's invitation. She looked excited and, to my surprise, accepted it eagerly. It surprised me because we have always spent Christmas together in the flat. In fact, it's always just been the two of us ever since dad died and I thought she would hate the idea.

Pushing aside any thoughts of Christmas, I reach for my books. Christmas will have to wait because getting through the next week is much more important.

2

"This is so difficult. I don't know the first thing about them so what on earth should I buy?"

I laugh to myself because, as usual, mum looks worried. "They won't expect you to buy them anything. Just some smellies or something along those lines."

Mum sighs and I leave her looking at the rows of boxed toiletries and head over to the make-up counter. We've been at the mall for hours now along with half of the population it would seem. Last minute Christmas shopping is never a good idea, and I regret agreeing to help mum buy some gifts for Oliver's family. She's right, it is the right thing to do, after all, you can't accept an invitation to stay at somebody's home for Christmas without taking your hosts gifts.

Finally, she decides on two toiletry sets and we make our way to the local coffee shop. As we head inside, I see the line to order is long and my heart sinks. Turning to mum, I say kindly, "Why don't you grab a seat and I'll order."

She fumbles in her bag and hands me some money, "Ok, but take this. You're still a student and can't be expected to buy me things when you need all the money you can get."

I know better than to argue, so I accept it graciously and study my phone as I wait.

Oliver has texted me six times since we arrived and I smile as I see the latest one.

I miss you sooo much. When will you be back?

I dash off a quick reply.
Another couple of hours I expect. What do you have planned for this evening?

I laugh as a massive love heart spins into view and there are no prizes for guessing what's on his mind. In fact, it's always on mine too. Don't get me wrong, we enjoy many nights out and get invited to most of the parties but the best nights are the ones we spend when it's just the two of us. More often it starts with a movie and a takeaway pizza and ends up in bed before the film even ends.

Oliver shares a house with three other students just outside the university. It's not cheap but his parents pay for him to live in comfort while he supposedly studies. He's lucky because he appears to be good at everything. He's amazing at sport and even aces his studies. He never has to try too hard which is why I'm a little behind. I'm not that lucky and have been neglecting my studies ever since I met him. I know my mum would be angry if she found out I was slipping and I feel bad. We've never had much money and I know she works two jobs to send me to university and I feel terrible that I'm failing because of my relationship.

Glancing over, I see her chatting to someone by the window and as I look again, I see Nancy laughing at something she is saying.

By the time I've been served and make my way across to them they are deep in conversation and look up slightly guiltily as I say, "Honestly, why does it take so long to make a cup of coffee these days?"

Nancy laughs as I grin. "Hey, babe. I didn't know you were in town. You could have shared a lift with us."

"Now you tell me. It took me ages to get here on the train but I forgot I needed to pick up a picture that I had made for my parents."

I note the large package at her feet. "What is it?"

"Me, of course. Who wouldn't want a picture of their pride and joy at Christmas?"

Mum laughs. "I would. I think it's a lovely present, Nancy. So thoughtful."

She frowns. "I still don't know what to get for Oliver's father though. Do you know if he drinks gin?"

I feel a little uncomfortable with Nancy listening and shake my head. "No, I don't think he drinks."

"What, at all?"

I shrug and try to change the subject. "I'm not sure but you can't go wrong with socks and a body spray. Shall we check out Boots after this?"

Mum nods and Nancy leans forward. "Listen, have you heard?"

"What?"

"Sadie Carmichael's pregnant."

I stare at her in shock and mum looks disapproving.

"Isn't she the girl who took your place on the debating team?"

I feel uncomfortable as Nancy grins. What mum doesn't know is that I gave up my place to spend more time with Oliver. I told her that Sadie had taken my place because they considered her better than me, so I just nod. "Yes, goodness, who's the father?"

Nancy shrugs. "Nobody knows but there are several rumours as you would expect."

Mum looks interested and I feel her disapproval from here.

Nancy loves nothing more than to gossip and whispers, "Millie Farmer found the ultra-scan in the bathroom bin. Apparently, Sadie was the last one in there and so it must be hers. When Millie asked her, she went completely mad and screamed the place down. Obviously, she didn't want that little secret to come out. I mean, she's been polishing that innocence of hers all the time she's been here but I've heard different."

I feel uncomfortable as mum leans forward and says in the same whisper, "What do you know?"

"Well, Lewis Butler told everyone he had her on the night of the Halloween disco. Do you remember, Lily, she was dressed as a devil and was last seen disappearing upstairs with him? Not so innocent after all it would seem. Maybe he's the

18

father, or maybe it's someone else entirely. They say the quiet ones are the worst."

Mum looks shocked and I feel a little awkward. It's one thing gossiping with my fellow students but the last thing I want is for my mother to see what life is really like on campus.

She shakes her head sadly. "That's terrible, the poor girl. She could ruin her life because of one reckless moment."

Nancy laughs. "I don't think it was just one Mrs Adams. Word is she's pretty wild under that twinset she wears."

She looks at her phone and groans. "Heavens, I must go. I'm meeting my brother in five minutes to help him choose a gift for mum. He's hopeless and we usually grab the first thing he sees. Anyway, see you later Lily, nice to chat with you, Mrs Adams."

We watch her rush outside and mum sighs heavily. "That poor girl, Sadie what's her name? I wonder what she'll do."

"Who knows, anyway, we should get going too. Time is pressing on and we need to finish this list."

As we walk away from the coffee shop, I think about Sadie Carmichael. She's a pretty girl but overly studious to the point of being a nerd. I don't blame her for having her head turned because Lewis Butler is another one considered quite a catch. He's on the team with Oliver and I know they don't get on. A little bit of rivalry that stems from the time Lewis hit on me at a party one night. He didn't know that Oliver and I had hooked up only the

19

week before and didn't really deserve the thumping Oliver gave him. As I think about that night, I feel the bad taste in my mouth returning. I don't like violence and especially not over me. Oliver was extremely apologetic afterwards and I know it was mainly the drink inside him talking but still. He's never lost control like that again which I'm glad about because I'm not sure if I could be with a guy who fights.

"Lily, darling, do you think I should get a new outfit to wear on Christmas day?"

Turning, I see mum holding up a beautiful green dress and smile.

"Yes, that's gorgeous, it suits you."

She heads off to try it on and I sigh inside. I wonder if this was such a good idea; I don't even know Oliver's family that well myself but they apparently insisted.

Another text flashes on my screen and I laugh at the picture of Oliver blowing me a kiss. At least he'll be there, that's the main thing, after all.

3

By the time we return home I almost don't have time for a cup of tea before I must leave to meet Oliver.

However, mum insists and as I wait in the familiar, comfortable kitchen that always seems to be full of love she says with interest.

"Tell me about Oliver's family. I should know a few things before I meet them."

"I don't know what to say, really. To be honest, I don't know them that well myself."

"He must have spoken about them, surely?"

Nodding, I take the mug of tea gratefully. "His mum doesn't work, she stays at home - you know, a housewife."

Mum looks a little irritated. "Why can't she work?"

I shrug. "I think she could if she wanted to but they are fairly well off so I don't think she has to."

Shaking her head, mum sits down on the opposite side of the table. "Well, it's not right."

"Why not?"

"Because women shouldn't let themselves be controlled by a man. They should earn their own money and have their independence."

Sighing, I try to dodge the conversation that's a favourite with her. "Anyway, for whatever reason, she doesn't work. His father's an accountant and

21

owns his own company. He works a lot which is why she probably runs the home. It takes the pressure off him so that when he gets home, he can relax."

I quickly carry on because from the look in mum's eyes she doesn't agree with that either.

"He also has a brother, Toby. He's a graphic designer and works in Leeds. I think he has a flat there but comes home to visit a lot."

"Does he have a girlfriend?"

"I'm not sure? Maybe."

Sighing, mum takes a sip of her tea and says rather irritably. "I'd better get another gift just in case he brings someone. It's terrible to be excluded on Christmas day of all days."

Setting my mug down, I say gently, "Listen, mum, don't feel as if you have to buy for everyone. For all we know, they could have hordes of relatives descending on them on Christmas day. They wouldn't expect you to bring a gift for everyone, so stop worrying about it."

She smiles but I can tell I haven't convinced her.

"So, what about his father, what did you say his name was?"

"David."

"Yes, David, why doesn't he drink gin?"

Resisting the eye roll her question deserves, I shrug. "Listen, Oliver told me they don't drink - any of them."

I feel her sharp stare stripping me bare and sigh. "If you must know, Oliver told me his dad has a drinking problem. Consequently, there is no alcohol allowed in the house. They don't drink around him and just make fabulous mocktails instead."

She laughs softly. "Mocktails?"

"Yes, non-alcoholic cocktails. That way they still have fun with none of the headaches afterwards."

Mum looks a little brighter and I can tell this is something she approves of.

"Anything else I should know?"

Standing, I smile and grab my bag. "If there is, I can't think of it. Anyway, I must go because I have work that needs finishing before our final week. If I'm to enjoy Christmas with a clear conscience, I should really get going."

She walks with me to the door and hugs me warmly. "Thanks for taking the time to spend with me, darling. You know I appreciate it, especially as you're working so hard. I'm incredibly proud of you, do you know that?"

I feel a pang as my mother hugs me and feel bad. I hate lying to her and I know she thinks I'm some super student but I'm not. I barely scrape an average mark and I'm so far behind I'm just surprised I haven't been summoned to the Dean's office to explain myself. The trouble is - Oliver. I just want him and when it's a choice between being cuddled up next to him in bed or swatting in the library, there's no choice. He wins every time and I can't shake the guilt that chokes me when my mother looks at me with so much pride in her eyes.

Feeling as if I'm suffocating, I pull away and kiss her on the cheek.

"Take care mum and don't work too hard."

She nods and as I turn to leave, she pulls me back and presses some money into my hand. "Here you go, darling. Just a little something to keep you well-nourished."

I make to give it back but she fixes me with the look that tells me not to even try and says briskly. "Now go and make your mother proud."

As I head back to Uni, I feel like the worst daughter living. She deserves someone like Sadie Carmichael, not me. I am the worst daughter in the world and have dug myself a hole that it's doubtful I'll make it out of alive.

4

The party's in full swing as we head inside and I feel the stares as we walk through the crowds. This is the last night of Uni before Christmas and everyone's out to get smashed. Being with Oliver is easy. He's one of the most popular guys on campus and as his girlfriend, I go where he goes. I know the other girls are jealous of me and I love that he's mine and has no problem showing his devotion in public. He is attentive, charming and caring and makes every other guy here look like a poor second best. The envious looks as he fusses over me makes my heart sing and when he kisses me in full view of everyone, I absolutely love it.

So that's why something feels different tonight.

For the first time since I met him, I am left on my own – a lot. In fact, as I stand chatting with my friends, I don't even see him leave the room. Looking around, I say to Nancy, "Did you see where Oliver went?"

She shrugs and looks behind me. "Nope, he's not attached to you by that invisible cord you tether him to. Maybe he's escaped."

Rolling my eyes, I try to look unconcerned. "He must be in the bathroom."

However, I find the conversation more stilted and the unease grips me as the minutes tick by and he still doesn't appear. After a while Nancy nudges me and I see Sadie Carmichael almost running down the stairs looking upset. "Wow, it looks as if someone's ruined her Christmas already. I wonder who?"

An uneasy feeling grips me but I shrug and look unconcerned. "Who knows?"

Looking around, I see Lewis Butler smooching with another girl on the dance floor and whisper, "I think there's your answer, look."

Nancy follows my stare and laughs. "I think you're right. Who's that girl he's with, anyway?"

"Lola Francis. I think she's studying drama."

Nancy laughs loudly. "She's come to the right place then."

I feel a hand snake around my waist and feel Oliver's lips brush my neck. "Here she is, my beautiful Lily flower."

His words are slurred and his breath stinks of alcohol making my heart sink. Nancy looks at him longingly and I feel a flash of irritation. Shrugging him off, I say loudly, "Nancy, do you fancy dancing with me?"

She looks surprised as, without a backward glance, I pull her onto the dancefloor.

"What's going on?" She says in a whisper as I dance as if I haven't got a care in the world. "He's drunk, and that's not good."

"Why, who are you, his mother?"

I don't answer her because I don't have an answer. He can drink himself into a coma for all the business it is of mine, yet something unwelcome

26

has taken over my reasoning and I know what it is – jealousy. I'm not sure why but Oliver's up to something. I know him so well and for weeks now I've sensed a change in him. He seems distracted and never leaves his phone unguarded. On the odd nights I've been studying I heard rumours of his partying and whispers of other girls. He denies it all but there's a part of me that's just waiting for him to cheat on me. It's the part of me that tells me I don't deserve a guy like him. I'm not in the same league and so, it's just a matter of time before he ditches me for someone who is. Sadie Carmichael perhaps. She certainly has money; her parents have a country house in the Cotswolds and their London residence. I know she holidays in Saint Tropez and goes skiing in Aspen. Yes, Oliver and Sadie should be together because that's what nature probably intended.

I try not to look but see his slightly wounded expression as he watches me from across the room. My heart lurches as I see a girl slide up to him and run her hand up and down his arm. I swallow hard as he half turns towards her and leans down as she whispers something in his ear and then his eyes find mine and an unspoken conversation passes between us. He knows and I know that he has the power to take that girl upstairs and there's nothing I can do about it. I feel sick as he laughs at something she says and stares at me with triumph in his eyes. I continue to sway to the music as if I haven't got a care in the world as I feel all eyes focused on us as the crowd senses a shift in the air.

Then I watch as he shrugs the girl's hand off his arm and says something to her that causes anger to flare in her eyes and a hurt expression to cross her face. Then he holds my eyes with his as he walks purposefully towards me, cutting through the crowd like a knife in butter.

I feel the intensity as he reaches me and pulls me towards him roughly before kissing me hard and fast.

Now there is nobody else in the room.

Now the music ceases to exist and now all is right with the world. Yes, Oliver is Lily Adams' guy and everyone knows it.

Waking up the next morning beside Oliver is a luxury we will have to forego over Christmas. If my mother knew I was sleeping with him, all hell would break loose.

I turn to look at the man who makes my heart beat faster and my principles desert me. He looks so perfect as he sleeps and I smile as I think back to last night. We left the party almost immediately and returned to his house. Sex with Oliver has always been good but last night it reached a new level. Maybe it was because of the friction between us or maybe it was because we know it's the last time until after Christmas but my feelings threatened to overpower me and we couldn't get enough of each other.

Now, faced with the thought of Christmas with our families, not for the first time I wonder how on earth I got so lucky.

5

As I straighten the cushion, I take a look around and sigh before checking the time on the clock. 11.00 am. Perfect.

Almost on cue, the doorbell rings and I smooth down the non-existent creases in my skirt as I head to answer it.

"Darling, you look amazing."

I air kiss my friend Celia as she pulls back and gushes. "I love your hair. Did you go for a new colour?"

"Yes, Giovanni thought I would look good with a few blond highlights. I'm quite pleased with it actually."

"So you should be, darling. It's taken years off you and is nowhere near as painful as the surgeon's scalpel."

She laughs in that high-pitched, annoying way she has perfected over the years and looks around her with a critical eye. I feel guarded as I try to see my home through her eyes and almost hold my breath as I see a crooked cushion and a speck of dust on the mirror. Celia's home is one hundred percent perfect. All the latest furnishings from the most expensive shops. On trend and bang up to date courtesy of the interior designer she appears to have

30

on a retainer. A home so immaculate you almost don't feel as if you can breathe for fear of tarnishing something.

I follow her into my kitchen because Celia follows no one. She leads and the rest of us trail behind her and as she casts her eye around the gleaming surfaces, I feel anxious as I wait for her approval. Turning to face me, she smiles and places her bag on the counter. "You must tell me what diffuser you are using. Such a delightful scent, very seasonal."

Moving across to make the tea, I smile with relief. "I always use Jo Malone. A little expensive but worth it."

"Hmm yes, it pays to buy the best. You can always tell. You know, I visited Virginia last week and saw one from Next in her downstairs toilet. Can you imagine putting that one on full view for everyone to see. She could have at least decanted it into the one I bought her from Harrods for her birthday."

Nodding, I pity Virginia. The poor woman has probably got a lot more on her mind than decanting diffusers to appease her visitors and I sigh. "I feel sorry for her."

"Why, just because her daughter failed her A levels and didn't get into Oxford? Some people always punch above their weight, anyway."

"No, because I heard Thomas could lose his job."

I note the sudden change in the air as Celia digests this new information that she has obviously not been privy to. "Is that a fact?"

I can almost hear the cogs turning from here as she absorbs what I told her and works out what it means for our friendship group. Only high achievers and people with a disposable income need apply. I pity Virginia because as sure as Christmas is coming, she will soon be struck off the intimate circle of friends we belong to if Thomas loses his job.

The doorbell rings again and my heart sinks. That's probably her now and I wish I hadn't said anything. Celia will no doubt be cool towards her and she'll know I'm the one responsible.

Excusing myself, I head off to greet her and as I open the door my heart sinks when I see the tears in her eyes. She moves inside and kisses me on both cheeks and I say softly, "Bad news?"

Nodding, she looks behind me and I raise my eyes in warning. She understands and smiles sadly before whispering, "Bad news I'm afraid. As of the new year, Thomas will be…"

She almost can't say the word and then whispers, "Unemployed."

Before I can comment, we hear, "Virginia, darling, how pretty you look in pink. Come through, it's been so long we really should catch up."

Throwing her a sympathetic look, I watch her head towards the eye of the storm knowing there is nothing I can do about it. Her fate is sealed and I feel bad for her. I wonder what this will mean for her family because I know that her house is mortgaged to the hilt. I hope they don't have to move because of all my friends she's the most genuine and I would miss her more than she knows.

I leave them chatting and concentrate on making the tea, making sure to arrange everything perfectly as is the norm at these gatherings.

The doorbell rings again and I head off to greet my final guest. Celia's best friend, Delilah Fortescue. I feel a shiver inside as I contemplate greeting a woman that makes my skin crawl. As I open the door it does just that as I see the botoxed, designer encrusted barbie doll standing there. She is wearing the largest fur coat I have ever seen outside Russia and yet she wears oversized sunglasses that make her tiny face look miniscule. Her bright red painted lips are bared in an insincere smile and I can tell she is assessing every inch of me behind her shades.

She smiles and steps forward, air kissing me as she goes before sweeping past and dropping her coat on the bannisters. "Darling, it's positively Arctic out there. Thank goodness your home is so warm and inviting."

I hear the shrieks of welcome from the kitchen as she reaches it and sighing, pick up her coat and place it in the cupboard nearby along with the rest, before braving the room before me.

It wasn't always like this. Celia never used to scare me when we first became friends. She was kind, funny and a little scatty if I'm honest. Then she met Delilah and appeared to change overnight. Suddenly, she became obsessed with material things and keeping up with the Jones's. Her bitchy comments stared to seep into the cracks of our friendship and take root. Like all bullies she rules with barbed retorts that strike fear in your heart that you will be on the end of them. I should have walked away but she makes it impossible to.

Sighing, I head inside to join them and imagine what will happen if Virginia does lose everything. I wonder what that would feel like?

By the time I have served the usual gluten free cake and mint tea, the conversation turns to Christmas and Delilah informs us she will be spending it at home before flying off to Verbier for the New Year. Celia squeals with delight as she interrupts, "Oh darling, I can't wait to join you." Turning to Virginia, she says happily, "Blake and I will be joining Delilah and Tristan in their impressive mountain chalet. What will you be doing for Christmas and New Year, Virginia?"

My heart sinks as I see the razor-sharp stare Celia throws her as Virginia squirms a little. "Just staying at home with the family."

Delilah shrugs, "Never mind. Maybe you could get away afterwards."

"Yes maybe." Virginia looks uncomfortable, so I say quickly, "I'm the same. We have quite a house full this year. Oliver's bringing his new girlfriend

34

home with her mother and they're staying until Boxing Day."

Celia looks interested. "Ooh, tell us about her, darling. Did you say mother, doesn't she have a father?"

"No, I believe he died when she was just a small child."

Virginia shakes her head sadly and Delilah says incredulously, "What and she never married again, shocking?"

Celia nods and I shrug. "Maybe she never met anyone."

"What does she do for money then?"

Delilah shares a look with Celia which annoys me and I snap, "Work, maybe?"

Virginia smiles sweetly as Delilah snorts, "Imagine that. Thank goodness we don't have to."

I listen to the laughter around me and my heart sinks. I'm not sure when I became this shallow person with no meaning to my life but I don't like it. When the boys were small, it was great knowing I didn't have to work and could devote all my time to caring for them. I loved being here when they came home from school and loved moulding myself into the perfect mother and wife. Now they've left I feel very redundant and I don't like it one bit. Everyone else has moved on with their life and I've been left right back where I've always been. Maybe that's why I've become this person that I hate.

Blinking away the tears that threaten to reveal how close I am to unravelling, I say brightly, "Yes, thank goodness. Anyway, would you like some more tea?"

Once my friends have left, I think about my life as I clear away the tea things. If I'm honest, I feel lonely and just go through the motions most days. Maybe Christmas is just what I need right now. It will be lovely to meet Lily's mother because Lily's such a lovely girl and I can see she makes Oliver happy. It strikes me that she's the first girl he's brought home and I remember thinking what a pretty girl she was when she sat nervously on the settee beside him. Oliver has always been good looking and quite dazzling in his personality. Lily is no exception with her pretty blond curls and baby blue eyes. She is a sweet girl and I feel happy that he's met her. I'm looking forward to meeting her mother and maybe it will good to surround ourselves with normal people over Christmas because one thing I already know about the new year, my life is going to change, I'll make sure of it.

6

Sighing, I join yet another line for the checkouts as I contemplate my basket brimming with pointless gifts just to tick another box. All around me people are looking stressed and tired as they do the same and try to bring some order to the usual festive chaos. Impatience is the feeling of choice these days as it appears that everybody in the universe seems to annoy me and only the sight of two small children running around excitedly reminds me why we do this at all.

Thinking about Christmas appears to be the milestone I need to reach before the rest of my life can begin. I have made a decision and I'm not sure if the rest of the family will like it but as soon as we pack away the Christmas decorations; I am looking for a new job.

David will probably make a fuss but I'm prepared for that. It's about time I put myself out there and explored what life will be like post children, pre-grandchildren, for Florence Buckland. I feel excited as I think about days filled with more than just polishing the counters until they sparkle and stressing over the pile of ironing that never seems to go away.

"Florence."

I feel a tap on my shoulder and a deep masculine voice gets my attention as I spin around in surprise.

Standing behind me is Blake, Celia's husband, and he smiles. "I thought that was you."

"Oh, hi Blake, this is unusual."

He raises an eyebrow. "What, seeing me out in the daylight? Yes, contrary to popular opinion, I don't live in a darkened, wooden box for most of the day contemplating my next victim when the sun goes down."

Laughing, I nod towards his basket. "Christmas shopping?"

"Hmm, nothing gets past you, does it? I must up my game."

He smiles sweetly to counteract the acid in his retort and sighs. "I hate Christmas."

"Why, because you actually have to do your own shopping for a change?"

"Busted." He laughs softly. "What about you, it looks as if you're giving Santa a run for his money?"

Reminding me I appear to have the contents of Santa's sleigh weighing down my arms, I groan. "Yes, I thought I had finished but then we had more visitors to accommodate. After this, I'm done though – thankfully."

As the line edges forward, we shuffle along with it and I think about Blake Cosgrove. I only know him through Celia and have only shared the odd polite word with him as we socialise at night. He appears to be a man's man and I often hear tales of his famous binges with his rugby club pals. Celia often bemoans the stench of stale alcohol contaminating her air when he rolls in during the early hours. This reminds me of David's problems and once again I feel bad for him. Because of his addiction to alcohol, he's removed himself from every situation that could destroy his resolve and consequently doesn't have the same tight group of friends as most of our neighbours enjoy.

Blake groans and looks at his watch. "Why does shopping take so long? I thought I'd only be thirty minutes - tops. It's been double that already."

Looking into his basket, I note with interest the pile of silken material and grin. "It looks as if you got distracted in the lingerie department."

His eyes sparkle and a mischievous grin flashes across his face. "Just a little something for the love of my life. I hope it fits because if I get this wrong, I will ruin Christmas."

Nodding, I see his predicament. Too big and Celia will fly into a rage with him for daring to think she is larger than she is. Too small and she will instantly feel depressed and forego Christmas dinner in favour of the Atkins diet with immediate effect. I roll my eyes and grin. "You're a brave man, I'll give you that."

"Substitute brave for stupid and I think you're spot on."

"Why risk it then?"

He shrugs and looks at the innocent items languishing in his bag. "Isn't this what women expect? If I bought her the new Dyson she's been banging on about, she would probably stab me with the carving knife instead of the turkey. If I bought her chocolates, she would accuse me of trying to sabotage her diet and if I bought her anything for the home, I would probably expect divorce papers to be served instead of Christmas pudding."

Laughing, I see his predicament. "It's still dicing with danger to choose clothing. What about jewellery or the latest designer handbag? You know, she adores perfume, maybe you could buy her some with a matching body lotion."

Blake groans and I see the light dim in his eyes. "Now you tell me. I've just spent way too long choosing this and now you've made me doubt everything."

I feel a little bad and say kindly, "Let me take a look. Maybe I could cast my 'best friend's' eye over your problem and give you my seal of approval."

Looking a little happier, he swaps baskets with me and says in surprise, "This basket is seriously heavy. Are you in training for some kind of weight lifting competition?"

"No, but it helps keep the gym membership costs down."

I take a look and note that the line is still moving slowly and say quickly, "Why don't I head over and see if I can find something she'd like. You keep our place and then we won't waste any more time than we have to."

Looking so grateful it brings a smile to my lips, Blake just nods and sighs as he stares at the scores of people in front of him.

As I walk back to the lingerie department, I think how lucky Celia is that he's trying at all. David is sure to give me money. In fact, he always does. No beautiful designer gifts for me, just a card with a wad of cash to spend in the sales. He always accompanies it with the usual, 'I never know what to get you and thought you'd prefer to buy it yourself when it's half price.'

I set the basket down and pick up the small scraps of fabric that pass as underwear and feel a pang as I see the sexy lingerie before me. Black silk and lace that looks nothing on the hanger but is sure to look a million dollars on Celia. Thinking of my own underwear drawer, I feel deprived. Practical bras and knickers designed for comfort rather than attraction. In fact, I could certainly use some new items because I can't even remember the last time I bought any. Quickly, I check the size and note that he has chosen one way too small. Shaking my head, I replace them and select the right size. Celia is definitely the same size as me and sadly we are definitely a few pounds heavier than we were in our youth.

Sighing, I turn towards the queue and battle my way through the padded bodies of the Christmas shoppers that are wrapped for an arctic winter while melting under the heat in the shops.

Blake smiles as I approach and I thrust his basket towards him. "Here you go, I swapped them for her size so you should have a stress-free Christmas. Maybe you should ask at the checkout if they have a gift box and then it will save you having to wrap it when you get home."

I make to swap baskets and he shakes his head firmly. "I'll carry this. It's far too heavy and is the least I can do after you saved my Christmas."

He grins and I laugh softly, "Well, if you insist."

As we wait, he says with interest, "So, how are things? It's been a while since we saw you, is David ok; what about the boys?"

"Oh, they're all fine. Oliver has a new girlfriend and Toby is enjoying his new job."

"And David… is he… um… well, doing ok?"

I feel a prickle of anger as I think about David. It's common knowledge among our friends about his problem and appears to be the focus of conversation every time we meet. Because of his weakness, we spend our lives living on a knife-edge waiting for him to slip up and fall off the proverbial wagon. "He's ok. Just getting by as best he can."

Blake looks sympathetic, and it makes me more annoyed than it should. I hate this and am resenting David because of it. I see the concern in Blake's eyes as he says softly, "Let me thank you for your help and buy you a coffee."

"Don't you have to get back?" I say in surprise because I thought he was on his lunch break. Blake works nearby in the solicitor's office. He's good at it which is why they have lots of money these days. Celia used to work but when he started doing so well, there was no need and she just enjoys spending his money instead.

He looks at me kindly. "It's fine. There's not a lot going on at the moment, anyway. The staff are more preoccupied with arranging the office party and drinking their way through the customer's gifts. It will be good to take some time out away from it all."

He appears kind and maybe because I'm feeling so low, I accept his offer gratefully. "That would be great, thanks. I could use a caffeine hit right now."

We finally reach the end of the line and as we pay, I feel happier than when I joined it. Blake's good company and I'm looking forward to sharing a coffee with him. When I turn to face him, he takes my shopping bags from my hands and says firmly, "Here, let me."

As we walk towards the coffee shop, I think we must look like any other couple out Christmas shopping. It feels good having company, and it feels good walking beside a man like Blake. Celia is so lucky to have such a thoughtful husband and I can't remember the last time that David and I did this. Yes, things are set to change next year because it's more obvious than ever they must. If I am going to survive another year of my marriage, I need to shake things up a little and breathe new life into it.

7

Coffee with Blake has opened my mind. As I put the shopping away, I think about how I felt when I sat across from him in the steamy coffee shop. He was good company, and I found myself laughing – several times, something I don't appear to do a lot of these days. When was the last time David and I laughed? I can't even remember when we last had a coffee date, let alone a real one.

Sighing, I am forced to face the truth of something I've been ignoring for some time now, David and I are in trouble and at a critical point in our marriage.

The sound of the key in the lock reminds me of the time and my attention turns to the daily routine of making the evening meal. I hear the front door slam and David's car keys hit the polished wood of the hall table. I listen as he sighs heavily and then hear the thud of his shoes as he drops them on the tiled floor.

Then I hear the rustle of his clothing as he makes his way to the kitchen and look up and say dutifully, "Hi, good day?"

He groans as usual and snaps, "What's good about dealing with endless spreadsheets and people's inadequacies?"

I say nothing and he groans. "You know, my life is shit."

Still I say nothing because these statements are not unusual. In fact, he says them every time he walks through the door and it irritates the hell out of me. I want to scream at him that his life is definitely *not* shit. His life is one of privilege compared to so many. He has a loving wife – ok a wife, an immaculate home in a desirable area, he has two gorgeous sons who are doing well and he doesn't have to worry about money. His health is good and we enjoy two holidays a year. No, his life is definitely not shit, and I am fed up hearing him moaning about it.

Instead, I pour him the non-alcoholic beverage that has become the norm and say cheerfully, "Never mind, Christmas is just a few days away and then you can relax and unwind a little. You have a week off and maybe we should plan a few days out after the dust settles."

"Days out, what are talking about?"

He sounds incredulous and I suppose as comments go, it was rather out of the blue. In fact, I can't actually remember when we had a nice day out and I shrug. "I was thinking we don't spend time together anymore. You know, you're always working and what with my commitments we do nothing as a couple."

If I am waiting for the electric lightbulb in his head to go off, I'm an idiot because he just says angrily, "Since when do I get time to relax and have days off? I work long hours and when I get home it's dark. I'm so knackered I can't think straight and

45

when I do get a weekend off, it's spent doing the endless list of jobs you expect me to carry out whenever I'm here. So, tell me, exactly when are we going to fit in this nice day out because I'm guessing you would much rather I complete any DIY before actually putting myself first for a change?"

Without waiting for a reply, he turns and says over his shoulder, "I'm going for a shower, how long before dinner?"

"Half an hour," I say dully and try to ignore the tears that are burning behind my eyes. So much for trying, it appears that one of us has forgotten that you need to work at a marriage and gave up trying years ago.

As we sit down to eat, David flicks on the television and the sound of the evening news fills the silence. The conversation died years ago unless you count the rage that spills from my husband in the form of words as he disagrees with just about everything the newsreaders says. Not only is the news depressing but so is he. He rants about every item on there and the only conversation he directs at me is to shout his opinion without waiting for my reply.

Eye contact was lost along the way of our marriage and now the only look he gives me is one of irritation and derision if I dare to ask him to do anything.

Pushing away his plate, he sighs heavily. "You know, that's never been a favourite of mine."

"What, Spaghetti Bolognese?"

He nods. "Yes, can't we have something else for a change? I don't know, maybe a paella or something more exotic."

"Paella, since when did you eat that?"

"Since I woke up one morning and realised I eat the same thing on a revolving cycle. Monday is shepherd's pie, Tuesday usually curry, Wednesday is some casserole or another, Thursday may be a quiche with salad, Friday is always fish and chips, Saturday usually some meal deal from the supermarket and Sunday is roast dinner. Stop me if I'm wrong but I doubt it."

I feel the rage building inside as I say in a tight voice, "Then what do you want?"

I think I want to punch him as he shrugs, "Something different would be good. As I said, paella, or something like that."

He must take my silence as acceptance because he says a little kindlier, "You know, we have several cookery books growing dusty on the shelves. Why don't you study them and make a menu plan? Run it by me and I'll add my opinion, you know, work as a team. I'm not expecting you to rustle up a gourmet meal every night, just ring a few changes from time to time, you know I'll support you."

I catch sight of the heaviest cookery book I own mocking me from the shelf behind him and fight the urge to bash it over his head. Instead, I say in a cool voice, "Ok then, if you insist, while I clear away this inadequate meal, why don't you browse through the books behind you and prepare a menu plan for next week? I'll shop for the ingredients and make the food but you decide what you want to eat."

He says nothing because the weather comes on and his attention returns to screen and after a few seconds says angrily, "Is it ever going to stop raining? You know, this weather seriously depresses me. I think I have that 'sad syndrome,' maybe we should think about emigrating somewhere that actually has sunshine for more than two months of the year."

Resisting the urge to scream and haul the cookery book through the television screen, I march out of the room and leave him to it. Instead, I pace around the living room and count to fifty under my breath before I can even calm down and think about what an idiot I married. I bet Blake isn't droning on about menus and weather depression. I expect he's making sex eyes at Celia over the gourmet meal she probably rustled up in between the mad sex they obviously had when he returned from work. I'm guessing she meets him in all sorts of sexy underwear and before they even have a conversation, they're at it like rabbits. Yes, Celia and Blake are *that* couple. The ones that wear a smug expression because they've discovered the secret of a happy marriage. They actually like each other and are probably still madly in love. Maybe David and I can get that back, maybe I'm judging him too harshly and it's not just him that needs to shake things up a little.

As I begin to calm down, I think about what just happened. Maybe David is right, and it's not just the meal choice that has become stale over the years. Perhaps I am just as much to blame and need to stop feeling sorry for myself and shape up.

As I sink back against the soft cushions of the settee, a plan forms in my mind. Maybe this is just what I needed to breathe some new life into our relationship.

As I straighten the cushion and step back, looking at my perfect room, I make up my mind. I put a lot of care and effort into making my home as best as it can be but zero input into my marriage. Now the seed is sown, I feel excited. Yes, tomorrow it begins. Operation, 'save my marriage' and I know just where to start.

8

My heart is beating so quickly I think I may be having a panic attack, a heart attack or a stroke. Pulling my trench coat a little tighter around me, I push my way through the revolving door to David's office and wonder what he will think of my idea.

All around me the workers are rushing around with places to go and people to see. I catch sight of my reflection in the polished marble wall and think how out of place I look among them. The bored housewife with only one thing on her mind - her family and how to save her marriage.

I approach the receptionist and she looks up and smiles. "May I help you?"

"Um… I would like to speak with David Buckland please."

"Do you have an appointment?"

"No, I'm his wife, I didn't think I'd need one," I laugh nervously, and she smiles looking interested. "Oh, it's lovely to meet you, Mrs Buckland. If you would like to take a seat I'll buzz through to his office and see if he's free."

As I take my seat, I feel a little foolish. What wife has to wait to be granted a word with her husband? I should have security clearance, or whatever it is the people need that allows them to just walk to the lift and punch the correct floor number to take them where they want to go. I wouldn't even know which floor to press, let alone know the actual office he works in.

As I lift the company brochure off the table in front of me, it strikes me how little I know of my husband outside our home. I knew where he worked but I have never been here. In fact, I feel bad as I realise, he's been coming here for the last ten years. Is this really the first time I've ever met him here? Now I'm seeing things clearly, I realise just how much to blame I am too. It's not just David - it's me. We have had no interest in each other's life for years now outside of the bedroom and even that is practically non-existent these days.

I look around and see the Christmas decorations tastefully arranged in their corporate setting. Laughter fills the reception area and workers swap cards and discuss the office party tomorrow night. I hear the light conversation and relish the buzz in the air. I've missed this. I used to work in finance and was the assistant to a hedge fund manager. I loved my job which is why I'm surprised at how quickly I gave it up when I fell pregnant.

I always imagined that I would return once the baby was born but then Toby came along and everything changed. My life was set, a full-time mother and wife. I wanted it, in fact, so badly I never gave it a second thought. Do I regret it, not in a million but now I want something back that I should never have lost sight of – my independence.

"Excuse me, Mrs Buckland."

I raise my head and see the receptionist calling me and I hurry over.

"I'm sorry, your husband has left for lunch already with a client."

My heart sinks and she smiles apologetically. "I'm sorry, would you like to leave a message?"

Shaking my head, I make to turn away and then blurt out, "Do you know where he's gone?"

She looks a little surprised and I can tell she is conflicted. She is probably under instructions never to give any information away but she appears to come to a decision and lowers her voice. "I'm not sure but you could try Vincenzos in the High Street. I know a lot of business meetings are conducted there because we have an account there."

Flashing her a grateful smile, I head back the way I came in. Maybe I'll surprise him there instead.

Joining the crowded pavement proves more difficult than I first thought and it takes a while to make my way to the High Street. I feel a little nervous about going there at all because David may be angry if I interrupt an important meeting. Then again, I'm curious because now I'm here, I want to see him in action. I want to know about this side of him and see a different side of the man I married.

I shiver as the cold wind blows, reminding me it's winter and think about David's throwaway comment regarding the weather. Maybe we can take a holiday somewhere hot and sunny. I would quite like that and who knows, we may even rediscover those feelings we once had.

It doesn't take me long to find Vincenzos and I smile at the warm, inviting restaurant that sparkles with fairy lights and a cosy atmosphere.

As I push my way in, it takes a moment for me to see if he's here and I almost think he isn't until I hear a voice that I recognise and something else that I don't - laughter.

Turning towards the sound, I see David sitting opposite a glamorous woman who is giggling at something he is saying. I watch transfixed as he throws his head back and laughs and I don't miss the animation in his expression. I feel intrigued because David looks more relaxed than I have seen him in a long time. He appears younger, freer and dare I say it - happier and that woman is the reason.

My insides twist in pain as I watch my husband happier in another woman's company than my own. He used to look at me like that – once. We used to laugh and enjoy hearing what the other had to say.

A waitress approaches me. "Would you like a table for one, madam?"

My heart sinks – a table for one. Yes, that would be about right because that's all I have these days - myself. Shaking my head, I turn to leave but then something snaps inside me. Why should I go? Why should I scuttle away in the shadows while my husband entertains another woman? No, I have come here for a reason and if it's the last thing I do,

I'm going to see it through. So, I just smile and point to David.

"It's ok, I'm here to meet them."

She follows my finger and looks surprised because by the looks of things, they've eaten already. Ignoring her expression, I head towards their table and feel my heart thumping with every step I take. As I near them, the woman notices me first and looks interested. Then David looks up and the surprise on his face almost makes me burst out in hysterical laughter. Scraping back his chair, he says in shock, "Florrie, is everything ok?"

I see the panic in his eyes and feel the anger building. Is that a guilty look; have I inadvertently stumbled on the reason why my marriage is failing so fast?

I say coolly, "No, nothing's the matter, I just thought I'd surprise you and ask you out to lunch. It appears that I was too late though."

He looks more shocked than if I told him I was pregnant with twins and gasps, "Surprise me? I can't believe it."

He shakes his head and the woman with him says in a calm voice, "Maybe you should pull up a chair for your wife."

He looks at her and nods. "Oh... of course, I'm sorry."

I stand impatiently as he hurries across and grabs a chair from a nearby table and holds it out for me to sit. As I do, I look at the impeccably dressed woman and nod. "I'm sorry, I don't think we've been introduced. I'm Florence, David's wife and you are…?"

She looks interested and holds out her hand. "I'm Estelle, a customer of David's. I'm pleased to meet you."

My nerves settle a little as I see the friendly curiosity in her eyes and feel a little better. I'm not sure what I thought she would say, maybe, 'Hi, I'm your husband's mistress, we must compare notes,' or, 'Hi, I'm also David's wife what a coincidence,' or even, 'Hi, I'm David's whore that he likes to screw over his desk once a week and then reward me with a slap up meal afterwards.'

David turns to me and says incredulously, "I'm so surprised. I don't think you've ever met me for lunch before, why today?"

"Why not?" I shrug and stare at him pointedly as Estelle interrupts, "Would you like us to order you anything, Florence? The food here is seriously good, isn't it, David?"

I feel a prickle of jealousy as I see the easy familiarity they share and feel like the outsider as I shake my head and say coldly, "No thank you. I just thought I'd say hi."

I can see that David is now looking decidedly uncomfortable and wonder why? Has he been caught out having a dangerous liaison and doesn't know how to handle it? Is he forming an excuse as we speak that would actually be believable, or is he about to come clean and admit to having an affair because it certainly looks that way from where I'm sitting? Instead, he smiles happily and shakes his head, looking at Estelle in disbelief. "Well, this is a nice surprise."

She smiles at him warmly before scraping back her chair and saying pleasantly, "Listen, I'll leave you both to it. It's been good to catch up, David and lovely to meet you Florence."

Turning to David, I see her throw a pointed look in my direction as she says firmly, "Talk to her, David and you know where I am if you need me."

Before I can even ask what she means by that remark she is off and I stare after her in total disbelief.

Then I look back at David who looks a little guilty before saying, "We need to talk."

9

I feel as if I'm on a rollercoaster that has slowly been climbing a great height. Before me is the edge that promises a frightening drop as I tip over the side. David looks as if he's working out the best words to tell me what's obviously been a topic of conversation between him and Estelle and I hold my breath as I wait for my life to change.

Instead, he nods towards the menu, "Would you like to order anything?"

I grab the menu, more as a lifeline than anything else, to give my mind time to catch up. What will I do if he wants a divorce? The realisation that I care surprises me more than anything else I've seen today and my voice shakes as the waitress heads over and I say politely, "Please may I order a small lasagne and a glass of sparkling mineral water?"

Smiling, she looks at David who adds, "Another coffee if I may and the bill."

As she heads off, I feel my heart thumping as David says in a softer voice than normal, "It's good to see you, Florrie, it's a nice surprise."

"Is it?" I can't keep the bitterness out of my voice and he obviously notices it because his eyes narrow.

"Yes, it is. Anyway, I had better put your mind at rest because I can see the assumptions you've jumped to, so I'll just come clean."

I can't even think of an angry retort and just hold my breath instead, as he says sadly, "We both know we are struggling, don't we?"

My eyes fill with angry tears as I anticipate the words he's about to say.

The waitress returns with the water and I grab it as if I'm dying of thirst and take a large gulp.

To my surprise, David reaches across the table and takes my hand in his and says gently, "Relax, Florrie, I'm not having an affair."

His words cause my shoulders to sag and I almost want to weep with relief as I say in a small voice, "You're not?"

Squeezing my hand tightly, he says sadly, "Estelle really is a client - a good one. I've looked after her account for at least five years now and we regularly meet up for lunch - just as the client and accountant, nothing more. However, we are friends which is why I respect her advice."

"What advice is that, David?"

A hint of steel creeps into my voice as I anticipate what he's about to say. Then he surprises me once again by saying in a low voice, "She's a sex therapist."

Resisting the urge to giggle, I say in awe, "Really, is that an actual business?"

Grinning, he leans a little closer. "A good one actually. She does very well at it, I should know, I file her tax returns."

I feel confused and blurt out, "Why should that concern us?"

"Because I hope you don't mind but we got talking about our own… um, sex life and it opened my eyes - a lot."

I can feel my cheeks burning as David throws something out there on the table that should have been discussed years ago. He looks around and then leans even closer. "Estelle says that she can help us."

"What do you mean, help us?" I whisper, as I lean even further forward to disguise my words from the surrounding public and am surprised to see the fire burning in David's eyes as he says huskily, "We need to liven up our sex life and she can suggest things for us to try."

We quickly break away as the waitress returns, saying loudly, "One lasagne. Would you like parmesan cheese?"

I shake my head distractedly, "No thank you."

"Black pepper?"

She thrusts the large grinder in my face and I try not to see it as the phallic symbol that immediately springs to mind and say hastily, "No, it's perfect as it is, thank you."

Then she hands the bill to David and says brightly, "Let me know when you're ready?"

He nods and I want to giggle as his mouth twitches and he says in a low voice. "Will you try? I mean, I don't want to make you do anything you'd rather not."

Faced with a decision to make, I realise my life has turned completely the other way from where I thought it was heading. Suddenly, I feel more alive than I have in years and I'm glad to note that the thought of exploring a new sexual avenue with David is a lot more appealing than I thought it would be. I feel the forgotten stirring of lust for my husband that has been buried under domestic life and non-communication and feel excited for the future.

I can feel my eyes shining as I nod. "Ok, what next?"

David's eyes light up and he looks so excited I almost want to laugh out loud. The years just fall away and we are teenagers again as he whispers, "I'll book an appointment with Estelle. She told me she's finished for Christmas but has given me some online links to read up on. Shall we take a look this evening?"

Nodding, I take a bite of my pasta and feel warm inside. Suddenly, my life doesn't seem as bleak as it did an hour ago. Now it has purpose and excitement. Maybe next year will change for us in a good way. Perhaps David and I are both back on the same page and can live again. I hope so because as I sit opposite my husband, all the old feelings come rushing back. There was a reason we fell in love and we just lost sight of it somewhere along the line.

I walk with him back to the office and we hold hands as we always used to. He chats happily all the way, telling me stories of his customers that make me laugh. I don't even notice that it's cold and just beginning to rain. I feel warm inside knowing we have a bright future to look forward to.

As we reach the revolving doors of the office block, David pulls me close and kisses me hard, in full view of the workers. As he pulls back, he growls, "Maybe next time you meet me, wear the trench coat and nothing else."

I feel a little shocked and blush as he kisses me again and then pulls away with a wink. "See you later, I'll be home at the usual time."

As I watch him leave, I feel something stir inside me that hasn't been there for some time and I can't wait for him to get home for a change. However, before I head that way, I have a particular purchase in mind that I need to make first and it's waiting in the lingerie department.

10

ALICE

I think I've thought of everything but just to be sure I check the items off my list.

Then I pack them away in my suitcase and wonder what I'll find when I get there? Lily speaks so highly of Oliver's parents and yet to my knowledge she's only met them once.

Thinking about Oliver, I feel my chest tighten. I didn't like him. He will never measure up and after the list of endless questions I threw at him he failed the test miserably. In fact, I almost feel a panic attack coming on as I remember why the test was even invented. It was just for this reason; Oliver was the reason I invented this test and I feel my blood pressure building as I think about the situation we are now in – because of *him*.

I only want the best for my daughter. I want the best life, the best opportunities and the best of everything for her future. It was the exact reason I did what was necessary to get it for her. I'm not proud of the choices I've had to make, but I made them for the best of reasons – *her*.

Thinking of my daughter always brings a smile to my face. She is perfect - she always has been. An angelic little girl with golden curls and big blue eyes. I have protected her throughout her life and anything that has ever threatened her well-being has been dealt with ruthlessly.

Now it appears I must dig deep again and diffuse this latest threat to her happiness. She has always been a gullible fool, and it was inevitable that her head would be turned by such a man. Oliver Buckland is the type of guy mothers and fathers warn their daughters about in the first place. Good looking, cocky and arrogant, thinking the world will fall at their feet while they step over it to get what they want. Well, not this time because he has chosen to play with the wrong doll. This one comes with protection and he's about to learn what that involves.

Humming to myself, I pack the final few things I need to ensure we have a happy Christmas. It was fortunate that the Buckland's extended their invitation because it will make this a lot easier.

The sound of Lily's key in the lock settles my heart. She's home.

"Mum, where are you?"

"Upstairs, darling, just finishing the last of my packing."

I hear her bound up the stairs and laugh to myself. There is nothing I love more than the sound of my daughter heading towards me like she's always done. Whenever she needs me, I am here for her and always will be. Occasionally, I have had to take steps to avoid a bad situation becoming an impossible one and this is no exception.

The door opens, and she heads into the room and into my outstretched arms.

"I missed you, mum."

As my arms fold around her, I feel my heart bursting with love for my perfect daughter. "I missed you more, darling."

She pulls back and I note the excitement in her eyes as she grins. "Are you ready for this?"

Nodding, I reach for my suitcase. "Of course, it should be fun."

As she grabs my other bag, I lead the way, and she follows as she always has. I wonder how she'll feel when Christmas is over? I'm sure it will be a difficult time but necessary. Thinking about her room made up and ready, I steel my heart for what's about to come. She will thank me in the long run because after all, I'm her mother and only have her best interests at heart.

Lily chats happily as we set off for the Buckland's home. It makes my heart lift as I hear the happiness in her voice and then she says, "Thanks for doing this, mum. It must be strange thinking of spending Christmas with strangers when it's always just been the two of us."

"Things change, darling. It's inevitable. I always knew that one day you would fall in love and the man in question would have his own family. I'm excited for you both and looking forward to meeting them."

64

After a short silence, she says nervously, "It will be ok, won't it?"

"Of course, why wouldn't it be?"

I can tell there is something on her mind and anticipate the question. She laughs nervously before saying, "You won't say anything to put him off me, will you?"

I laugh out loud. "Why would I do that, when have I ever done that to you?"

"Well, there was Callum Evans. He told me that you told him I was seeing someone else. He never trusted me after that."

"Rubbish. Why would I ever say such a thing? I only want you to be happy, although he wasn't ever going to be the one to do it."

"Why?"

"Because they arrested him for raping that girl in the sixth form, don't you remember?"

Lily says in a shocked voice, "It wasn't him, the girl made it up, she admitted it."

I feel my blood boil as I remember it and say harshly, "Men like that always blame the woman. Of course, he did it, he was just let off because it was her word against his. No, there was no way on earth he was suitable for you."

I sense the unease in the air as she says tentatively, "What about Harrison Smith? He wasn't a rapist, but you reported him to the police for drink driving."

Shrugging, I inspect my fingernails. "He was going to drive you home, wasn't he? If you thought I was ok with that you are mistaken."

"But he only had one."

I snort. "One too many when you are in charge of a young life. No, Lily, I do not regret my actions because where you're concerned there are no red lines. I will not let anyone play with your well-being while I am alive to protect you. Anyway, Oliver hasn't put a foot wrong – has he?"

Quickly, she rises to his defence. "Of course not, he's the perfect boyfriend."

"Well then, you have nothing to worry about."

The music in the car disguises the awkward silence and I stare at the speeding landscape as it passes in a blur. Yes, Oliver Buckland is perfect in every way and just as imperfect. What Lily doesn't see through her rose-tinted spectacles is the flaws in the man she idolises. She doesn't see the imperfections that cause the cracks to appear and doesn't see the future as I do. Oliver is the boyfriend from Hell as far as I'm concerned and I will take great pleasure in ruining their budding relationship before it does lasting damage.

Feeling quite excited at the prospect of Christmas, I smile to myself. Such a happy time of the year, I am going to enjoy this one.

11

We pull up outside an impressive house set on a desirable street. I look around with interest at the houses I will never be able to afford in my lifetime and look forward to meeting the occupants.

We park behind a brand new 4x4 and Lily says softly, "That's David's car, Oliver's father. He's an accountant and does well from it."

Looking up at the huge house, I can see that he does. "How many bedrooms do you think it has?"

"Six, I believe."

"Why do they need six when there's only four of them and two only visit at that?"

Lily shrugs. "Because they can I suppose."

Noting the Christmas lights hung neatly under the eaves, I can tell this place has left nothing to chance. I expect the interior is dressed impeccably for the festive season and I picture our own small flat on the poorer side of town. I'm guessing the people inside this house don't even know how the rest of us live and I instantly despise them for their naivety.

Lily sounds nervous as she says hesitantly, "Shall we go inside?"

"Of course, that's why we're here, after all."

As we make our way up the long drive towards the front door, I wonder what my life would have been like if I had married into money. Would I still be the same person I am today, principled and unforgiving? Probably, because I have a strong moral compass that never bends. Even if I had money, I doubt I would waste it, unlike these people who appear to have recreated every single magazine spread on Christmas I have ever seen.

A pre-lit wreath hangs proudly from the front door knocker and I can tell it cost a pretty penny. The whitewashed wood looks as if it's cleaned daily as it dares any cobwebs or dirt to set up home on it. Silver lanterns contain church candles underneath an impressive porch and a metal bench holds various metal decorations entwined with ivy and festive foliage. From each window of the house shines a glittering wire star and the fairy lights twinkle enticing you inside. Warm lights shine from the window and from the main one a Christmas tree groans under the weight of immaculate decorations.

Yes, the Buckland's have it all, or so it would seem. I am looking forward to meeting them.

We ring the doorbell courtesy of a rope and a bell that hang to the side and Lily smiles nervously. We hear footsteps approaching and as the door swings open, a rush of warm air escapes scented with cinnamon and orange. Oliver stands there smiling happily and the look he gives Lily couldn't be loaded with any more love than it is. Impressive, I'll give him that.

He turns to me and smiles warmly. "It's good to see you, Mrs Adams."

"Call me Alice, please."

He smiles and takes hold of our cases and steps to one side. "Come in and meet my family."

We step into a large, impressive hallway and as expected this too is like a show home. It feels warm and welcoming and the surfaces gleam around us. Tasteful Christmas decorations are carefully placed and a garland twists around the impressive staircase, twinkling with lights and white satin ribbons.

As I shrug off my coat, a woman appears from another room and says happily, "Welcome, it's lovely to finally meet you, Alice isn't it?"

I look with interest at Florence Buckland and see a pretty woman with shoulder-length brown hair, streaked with blonde highlights, shaped in a blunt cut that frames her face perfectly and offsets her smoky grey eyes. She is well dressed and I can tell that her dress probably cost a small fortune.

"I'm pleased to meet you, Florence. Thank you so much for the invitation."

"It was our pleasure. Christmas seemed the perfect time to get to know you both." She laughs softly, "Although Oliver can hardly speak of anyone else, so I feel as if I've known Lily for years already."

Lily grins and I can tell she likes Florence. In fact, there is nothing not to like because she appears to be as perfect as her house. I catch Oliver wink at Lily and see the arrogance of a boy who has had everything handed to him in life. Outwardly he may appear perfect but I'm sure that if you cut deeply enough, the blood that spills would be tainted and rotten inside.

Florence ushers us into a large room and I look with interest at the comfortable silver sofas and gleaming modern furniture that is set on a light coloured, deep pile carpet. Scatter rugs create a warm environment and I see many polished silver frames with black and white photos of the family, all obviously professionally done.

Florence points to the comfortable chairs and says brightly, "Please make yourselves at home and I'll bring you some tea. Is that ok, or would you prefer something else?"

I smile politely, "Tea will be lovely."

"Ordinary, or I have decaf or mint tea, in fact, any kind of tea really, just state your preference."

"Ordinary will be fine."

Lily nods and Florence laughs. "Sorry, one more question, do you have normal milk or soya? I have dairy-free if you're intolerant."

I think I'm losing the will to live as I say lightly, "No, just ordinary everything. That's us, just your ordinary kind of girls."

Florence smiles and heads off to what I'm sure is a designer kitchen and Oliver sits awkwardly on the chair opposite a roaring fire, beside which burn two large church candles.

There's an awkward silence before Lily says, "Did you finish all your work before term ended?"

He nods. "Yes, what about you?"

"Yes, of course." She thinks I don't notice the flush creep over her face as she answers him. I also notice that she doesn't look up and immediately know she's lying. That irritates me more than anything because it means she is behind on her work but I remain silent. Now is not the time to bring up her course, there will be plenty of time to put that right later when we return home after Christmas.

As Florence makes her way back into the room carrying a large tea tray, the door opens in the hallway and closes almost as quickly. Florence looks up and smiles. "That will be David. He's been finishing off some work in the study so he can relax over Christmas knowing it's done."

As she pours the tea, I look at the man who enters the room. He smiles his welcome and I stand as he moves across to shake my hand. "Welcome, I'm David, you must be Alice."

I nod as he turns to Lily and winks. "Hello again, Lily, I'm glad you came because now Oliver will be on his best behaviour."

Oliver groans and Florence laughs. "It's started already."

She grins as she hands me my tea and as I take the dainty, bone china mug, I think about my own ones that were a bargain in the local discount store. It annoys me that I'm even comparing my life to hers because I've never been one who wanted material things. However, faced with the image of domestic bliss and perfection, I am starting to realise its power.

We all settle down and drink our tea while sampling some homemade biscuits that reinforce my impression of the woman who made them. Florence is a woman whose life is defined by what I see around me. I'm guessing this house and its occupants are her entire world which makes me feel a little bad about what I must do. However, I can't dwell on that because Lily is and always will be, the most important thing in my life and these people will learn what that means – the hard way.

12

"Let me show you to your room."

Florence smiles and I think how pretty she looks. I suppose I had an image of her in my mind before we came but she is nothing like I imagined. She seems softer, kinder and more approachable than I thought, yet there is something lurking underneath the surface and I can't put my finger on what it is. I wonder what I would find if I scratched that surface? Maybe she's made of stronger stuff than I think she is, only time will tell.

Lily remains behind and I can tell she is itching to spend time with Oliver. I didn't miss the loaded looks they shared and I'm not stupid, it's obvious their relationship is more developed than I first thought.

As I follow Florence up an impressive staircase, I try not to be jealous of the cosy, comfortable, yet elegant home she has created. We reach the top of the staircase and it branches off at the top. Florence waves to the right, saying lightly, "Our room is down the hall at the end along with two more of the bedrooms. The boys have those rooms and I have put you and Lily in the two at the other end of the house to give you a little privacy."

She stops outside the first room and smiles brightly. "We converted this room into a cinema room. It's been a godsend for the boys because it meant they could have some space from us and vice versa."

She opens the door and as I peer past her; I see a fairly large room with the biggest television screen I have ever seen in my life. It almost covers the entire wall and I feel a pang of envy as I see the comfortable settees arranged in an L shape, with a huge coffee table in front of them. In one corner of the room is a bar area which I can see is crowded with glasses and a popcorn machine.

We step inside and Florence says kindly, "Please consider this yours for your stay. You can chill out here away from us if you need to and grab some alone time."

She points to the bar. "Help yourself to drinks or snacks. There's a fridge under the counter and I've stocked it with various things I thought you may like. There's also a coffee maker and a kettle should you just want a hot drink."

I note the lack of alcohol and almost as if she read my mind, she sighs sadly. "I'm afraid this is an alcohol-free house. I'm not sure if Lily told you but we don't allow alcohol in here. I hope that's ok with you because it includes our meals and you may not like the thought of a dry Christmas."

Shaking my head, I smile. "That's perfect because I don't drink either. Never had and probably never will."

Florence looks interested and I laugh softly. "My ex-husband liked a drop or two and to be honest, got carried away. It got a little out of hand sometimes and caused so many problems in our marriage."

"I'm sorry, I didn't know."

Sighing, I sit down on one of the softest seats I have ever experienced, and she joins me. "It's hard sometimes dealing with addiction. Peter was just that you know, an addict."

"How did you deal with it?" Florence says in the saddest voice I have heard for some time and I smile sympathetically. "We just took one day at a time. We dealt with it as best we could but ultimately it wasn't enough."

"What do you mean, what happened?" I can tell Florence fears my answer because her situation is much the same. She must see the expression in my eyes because she says hastily, "I mean, you don't have to tell me or anything, I don't mean to pry."

Shrugging, I say in a sad voice, "Peter died of a heart attack. The drinking never helped his health, that's for sure but it was his heart that failed in the end."

"I'm so sorry."

Looking around me, I lower my voice. "Don't be, I had a miserable life with him. I lived my life on a knife-edge unsure what he would do next."

Florence looks shocked. "What did he do?"

I feel the pain almost choke me as I remember the man I married. The weak, despicable man who ruined my life. I feel the pain ripping at my heart and tearing it open revealing an infected wound that will never heal because of the rot that's set in. I am taken back to a time I would rather not revisit and say in a broken voice, "He was violent, Florence. He would get drunk and it dulled every inch of his reasoning. He would fly off the handle and break things against the wall. He would smash up the furniture and destroy anything in his path. He was a monster and deserved to die because the life he lived was hell unleashed from the bottle he drank from. So, in answer to your question, Florence. I don't drink and never have because I've seen first-hand what it can do."

Florence looks shaken and I know she's comparing it to her own situation. I look at her with sympathy and whisper, "I'm sorry. I know a little of your circumstances and I'm sure they are nowhere near as bad as my experience. It appears that your own situation is under control and I'm happy for you. Take no notice of me because I am bitter on the subject. However, if you ever need to talk, I am always happy to listen. I never had that friend who I could share my worries with. I had to deal with it on my own and it was hard. So, don't worry about us and just relax and try to enjoy your Christmas. It must feel a little awkward having strangers in your home for what is essentially a family time. I just want you to know that we both appreciate it very much and will try and muck in, so don't feel as if you must wait on us all the time."

Florence visibly relaxes and smiles, which makes her whole face light up. "Thank you, Alice. You know, I was a little apprehensive but I'm glad you're here. Lily is a gorgeous girl, and we are thrilled that Oliver has found somebody so nice to keep him out of mischief."

She laughs and I join her, although it grates a little. Oliver and mischief appear to go hand in hand and it's my job to make sure Lily knows that. I feel a little bad for Florence though. She appears an innocent in a house full of guilt and I wonder if she will be strong enough when the whole pack of cards comes crashing down.

She jumps up and grins. "Anyway, we've been distracted. Let me show you to your room."

I follow her along the hallway to a couple of doors side by side at the end of the house. She opens the first one and I see a pretty room decorated in blue and white looking as if it belongs in Homes and Gardens. It smells wonderful and I can tell it will be no hardship staying here for a few days. I drop my case to the floor and she says quickly, "I don't know if you've heard of a Jack and Jill bathroom but through this door is a fully equipped bathroom with a walk-in shower and roll-top bath. The other door leads to Lily's room, so you both have access to the same bathroom from your rooms. Is that ok with you?"

I smile gratefully and note the luxury of a bathroom that appears never to have been used. "It's perfect, thank you."

I see our reflections in the huge mirror that reflects the modern tiles and chrome fittings. Glass shelves hold bottles of interesting liquid and oils and a huge jar of soaps sits beside a pile of fluffy white towels. The air smells clean and inviting and once again I am impressed by the trouble this woman has gone to in making us feel comfortable.

Florence coughs nervously and says brightly, "Anyway, I'll leave you to unpack and settle in while I head downstairs to prepare the dinner. Don't rush, take things in your own time and at your own pace; I want you to feel at home here."

As she turns to leave, I say quickly, "Thank you, Florence. For everything. You are very kind."

She just smiles sweetly and heads back downstairs and I think about the woman I haven't seen for several years.

As the door closes, I can tell she didn't recognise me. I almost didn't recognise her, but that's understandable. She's changed significantly from the scared woman who came into my life almost twenty years ago.

As the memory resurfaces, I make a fist with my hand and feel the pressure of the past descending on me like an unwelcome virus.

Pushing it away, I take a few deep breaths and switch my mind to Lily instead. It's a coping mechanism I've perfected over the years because I need to forget the past and just concentrate on the future - my future with my daughter. Not the past, no that's an unwelcome memory that needs to be forgotten.

Humming to myself, I head back to the pretty blue and white room and start unpacking my things carefully, making sure to only remove the items I need immediately. Yes, this Christmas will be an interesting one, I'm quite looking forward to it.

13

Lily bounds into my room half an hour later and I laugh at the excitement on her face as she jumps onto the bed and grins. "This place is amazing, isn't it, mum?"

I nod and she babbles on. "Oliver is too, do you agree, please say you do?"

Again, I just nod and feel bad as I see her face fall a little as she says anxiously, "What?"

Shaking my head, I sit beside her and take her hand in mine and say softly, "I can tell he makes you happy, darling, and that makes me happy, but…"

"But what?"

I see the alarm in her eyes and I lower my voice. "It's nothing really and I shouldn't have listened to such obvious juvenile gossip."

Her worried eyes steel my resolve because even though I hate upsetting her, I hate what could happen more, so I sigh. "Nancy told me she was worried about you."

"Me?"

"Yes, she told me you had fallen hard for Oliver and she felt bad about the things she heard about him."

I see her bottom lip tremble and put my arm around her shoulders, saying kindly, "It's probably nothing but she told me there were quite a few rumours about him seeing other girls. Apparently, it's common knowledge around campus and the only one out of the loop, shall we say, is you."

The tears in her eyes threaten to spill and she says in a quivering voice, "But we are together all the time, he couldn't cheat on me."

Her words irritate me and I say sharply, "What about when you're studying. I'm pretty sure he's not with you then, or is he?"

I watch her cheeks redden and already know the answer to something I've suspected for some time. As she shakes her head, I feel the rage building as she lies to me. "This Sadie Carmichael, what do you know about her?"

Lily looks worried, "Nothing much, she studies hard and is getting a bit of a reputation, that's all."

"Hmm, Nancy told me that the other students are thinking the pregnancy test could have the result of a fling with Oliver, what do you think?"

Lily gasps and says in a shocked voice, "Rubbish, of course it wasn't Oliver."

She falls silent and I can hear her mind processing the information I have just fed her as the clock ticks on the wall beside us.

After a few minutes, I say brightly, "Of course it wouldn't be his. Why on earth would he want someone else when he already has a beautiful girl like you beside him? You know, I've seen this so many times in the past. The popular guy gets the prettiest girl in school, college, whatever and then puts her on a pedestal and screws around behind her back. You see, men are all the same, dear, they want their cake and eat it too. He is keeping you pure and innocent because he's a hypocrite. He wants the loyal, virginal girl as his future wife, someone he can mould and manipulate into the version of a woman he thinks he deserves and then gets his kicks out of sleeping with every other girl that allows him to satisfy his carnal urges."

Lily jumps up and I can tell I've gone too far when she hisses, "Don't speak about him like that. Oliver is not that person you describe, he just isn't. He is kind, loving and considerate and would never cheat on me. I don't believe a word that Nancy says and she's just jealous, anyway. All the girls want Oliver because he's the best at everything. The best looking, good at whatever he does, good company and kind and considerate. If Nancy told you stories about him, they are just that – stories. She also wants us to fail so she stands a chance of being with him. I'm surprised at you, mum, I always thought you had better judgement than to listen to childish gossip. Anyway, I need to unpack so I'll see you downstairs."

She flounces off and I shake my head. Yes, I was a little harsh and probably laid it on a bit too thick but I know my daughter. My words have angered her but the seed of doubt has now been sown and with a few more gentle prods in the right direction, my job will be done. Thinking about our chance meeting with Nancy, I realise how lucky we were.

That gossip was a delicious little titbit that I have manipulated to my advantage.

Once again, I hum to myself as I freshen up in readiness for the evening ahead. This trip will certainly prove interesting and I can't wait to see where it all leads.

Lily keeps her distance, so I venture downstairs an hour later and hear voices in the kitchen and head that way. I see the familiar easiness of a couple who have been married for some time as David pulls away guiltily from his wife and she grins. "Alice, I hope you've settled in."

"Yes, thank you, it's all very comfortable."

David smiles. "Can I fix you a drink, we have some superb cranberry fizz?"

"Thank you, that sounds great."

As I look around the huge state-of-the-art kitchen, I feel envious of a lifestyle I never thought I wanted – until now. It appears that David and Florence Buckland did very well for themselves over the years and are reaping huge rewards. As David hands me the glass he says cheerily, "Happy Christmas, and may it be a good one."

He hands a glass to his wife and I see the loaded look they share and once again feel a little disgruntled. How can a couple have everything, even after all these years? It's not fair, especially when I think of the direction my own life took.

Pushing my jealousy aside, I say brightly, "Please, allow me to help."

Looking a little surprised, Florence nods and pushes a bag of potatoes across the huge island unit she is prepping the vegetables on. "Thank you, maybe you could peel these for me."

As I take the knife, I note the gleaming sharp blade of a product that looks expensive. Hmm, Sabatier, a good make. As I cut through the skin, I relish the power of the blade and enjoy executing my task with as little waste as possible.

Florence is chopping some carrots and says lightly, "It's Beef Bourguignon, I hope that's ok?"

Nodding, I savour the smells of the beef cooking in the oven and note the soft lights of the candles burning on various surfaces around the room. "You have a lovely kitchen, Florence."

"Thank you." She looks pleased, and it's no wonder. This kitchen is obviously top of the range. Painted off white wooden units, with silver granite tops. A huge AGA taking a central position, set inside a huge fireplace with a large shelf above it. Soft closing cupboards and pull out drawers, neatly arranged. Chrome fittings on a butler sink and the biggest double fridge and freezer crammed full of delicious treats. The island unit dominates the room at which are three cream coloured, plush velvet stools. The floor is obviously Italian marble and there are beautiful festive flower arrangements mingling with the fairy lights providing the decorations. Across the room is a glass table, around which cream coloured, button back, dining chairs are placed. A huge real Christmas tree stands in front of bi-fold doors, with glittering white presents underneath, tastefully decorated with mistletoe and white satin ribbon. Even the gifts under the tree are colour coordinated with the kitchen and it all seems a little surreal and alien to anything I'm used to. Thinking of my own bargain wrapped presents waiting upstairs, I very much doubt they will be welcomed under the designer tree before me. Like Lily and I, they will look wrong against the background of privilege and be shown up for the imposters they really are.

David heads outside and I watch Florence follow him with her eyes and note the love shining from them. She catches me looking and smiles a little self-consciously as I say gently, "What's your secret?"

"My secret?"

Laughing, I nod towards the door he used. "How is it that after close on twenty years, you are still as loved up as you probably were at the beginning?"

Florence grins and lowers her voice, "Between me and you, Alice, it's all a bit new. David and I were going through a bit of a rough patch and then, only a few days ago, we discovered what the secret ingredient to a happy marriage really is?"

I'm intrigued and lean a little closer as she giggles, "Sex. Lots of it in fact."

She laughs at my expression. "I've shocked you, haven't I?"

I feel a little uncomfortable at the easy way she speaks of a topic so intimate and nod. "A little I suppose."

"Well, a few days ago I would have been too if I'm honest but when David suggested we see a sex therapist to help get our marriage back on track, I was a little taken aback at first. Then as I thought about it, I realised it could be just what we needed."

Sighing, she grabs her drink and after taking a sip, says in a low voice. "You see, things have been difficult for years. I suppose it was when David's problem got a little out of hand, we never really recovered from it."

I feel very interested and smile encouragingly. "I know how hard that would have been."

She nods. "It was a dark time and I'm amazed we pulled through at all but now it's as if that happened to two other people. I suppose David and I grew apart and stopped communicating. Well, we looked into the sex therapy and it lit a flame in our marriage that had almost burned out."

Slightly self-consciously she whispers, "Now we can't get enough of each other. Between me and you, I'm glad it's Christmas because I could do with the rest."

I shake my head sadly and she looks troubled. "What's the matter, have I shocked you?"

"A little but it's not that."

"What is it then?" She looks concerned and I say kindly, "Well, you say that David has an addiction to alcohol."

Her face falls and I say reassuringly, "That's fine, he is obviously dealing with it in the right way and with you and your family's support he's progressing well. He seems happy and content and I know more than most how easy it is to fall off the wagon as they say. I mean, maybe I shouldn't say anything but…"

I break off and she says in a worried voice, "No, please, I'd like to hear what you think."

Sighing, I place the knife down and whisper, "David is an addict. It's a fact and that brings with it a whole set of unseen problems."

Florence looks so worried I almost want to laugh out loud. "Well, from what I've heard, addicts usually swap one addiction for another. They're compulsive people and need to have something to fill that void in their lives. Some have affairs, some steal, some start collecting things, or binge eating. Anything to distract them from what they really want, which in David's case is alcohol."

Ignoring Florence's shocked expression, I press on. "Anyway, unless you handle this carefully, David could become a sex addict. Not a bad thing I suppose but when the other person in the relationship isn't one, the addict starts looking elsewhere for their fix."

I feel bad as Florence looks terrified and whispers, "He wouldn't - no, I don't believe he's addicted to sex, far from it in fact."

Pushing the bowl of potatoes away, I smile. "Of course, take no notice of me, Florence. You see,

I've always been one to speak and then think. Ignore what I've said and just enjoy the new relationship you have with your husband. I'm just being silly."

Florence smiles and I can tell I have now replaced the happiness with worry. Thinking about my own relationship, I wonder if things would be different now if Peter and I had seen a sex therapist. To be honest, I couldn't care less because I decided a long time before he died that I couldn't stand the man, anyway. Though maybe if he looked like David, it would have been a different story.

14

Dinner is a relaxed affair and I take my time to study the family. Florence and David are good company and Oliver is sweet with Lily who can't disguise her devotion to him. On face value, they appear to be the perfect couple and ordinarily I would be happy that she found such a man, however, fate has delivered a knockout punch, and it's up to me to clear this mess up.

After dinner, we watch a Christmas movie and then I make my excuses and head off to bed. I need time on my own to formulate my plan because I don't have long.

As I get ready, I feel the huge weight of responsibility weighing me down as I think about my daughter. I love her so much and it terrifies me to think of anyone hurting her. What terrifies me the most is that I will be the one she looks at with hurt and disappointment. She must never find out what I have done to keep her safe and so, as I battle the demons that plague me every day of my miserable life, I fall into a fitful sleep.

"I'm leaving you, Alice. I've met somebody else and I want a divorce."
His words register but I can't take them in. I feel the rage building like the blackest storm as I contemplate what he is telling me.

Leaving... me! He can't, I won't allow it.
Looking up, I stare at him with pure hatred and
snarl, "No!"
He shakes his head. "You don't have a choice. I'm
in love with another woman and fell out of love with
you a long time ago."
The rage overpowers my mind and I lash out,
screaming with rage as I hurl a vase against the
wall. The glass shatters along with my marriage as
I scream, "You bastard, no - I won't allow it."
"Calm down, Alice. Lily may hear you."
"How dare you remember you have a daughter?
How dare you consider her feelings above mine
when you are leaving us for a whore?"
I gasp and try to take in oxygen while my brain
scrambles to make sense of what he's telling me.
He says angrily, "Melissa is not a whore. She's
kind, gentle and loving, everything you're not."
My yell of rage propels me towards him as I slap
him hard across the face and rake my fingers down
his cheek. He tries to grab my hands but I punch
him low in the groin and he howls with pain and
falls to his knees. Gripping his hair, I twist it as he
cries out in agony and hiss, "You will never leave
me."
Spying a paperweight on the side table, I reach for
it but he pushes me aside before I can grab it and
restrains my wrists, yelling, "Stop it, you're mad."
Laughing hysterically, I feel the tears running down
my face as my life changes direction. Shaking his
head, he pulls me against the wall and holds me by

90

my throat, snarling, "I don't love you and haven't for some time. You're a wicked woman, Alice. You need help and I can't deal with you anymore. I don't want to fear what mood I'll come home to every night. I don't want to answer your twenty questions about what I've done with every hour of my day and I don't want **you***! Give this marriage up because it's not working. I'll always be a father to Lily and will make sure she is cared for but I need to leave for my own sanity."*

He releases me and as I slide down the wall in tears, I hear him leave, slamming the door behind him angrily.

Peter's had a heart attack.

The words take a minute to sink in and the voice on the other end of the phone says quickly, "I'm sorry, Alice, did you hear me?"

I manage to croak, "Yes."

The nurse from the hospital we both work at says kindly, "He's in ICU and I'm sorry, Alice but you need to get here quickly."

Slamming the phone down, I set about preparing myself to see my husband for the first time since he walked out yesterday. I can't believe this has happened. It's all happening so fast I can't deal with it. When he left, I cried all night long. How could he do this to us - both of us? He is leaving us to live with another woman and everyone will know.

I feel the whispers all around me.

91

As I walk the hospital corridors, it's as if they are closing in on me. I see the pointed looks and pity on the faces of my colleagues and with a heavy heart know just who's responsible.

The tears sting along with my bitter thoughts as I know just who they are thinking of – Peter.

Peter is a doctor at the same hospital and his indiscretions are becoming a problem I can no longer tolerate. We married after a blissful, whirlwind romance and shared many intimate liaisons in empty rooms and places we shouldn't have been. He was exciting and handsome and hooked and reeled me in with ease. However, almost as soon as the honeymoon was over, he lost interest. It's been five years of mental torture as I battle with his indiscretions. The proverbial lipstick on his collar and stale perfume on his shirts. The late nights that definitely weren't because of the hours he works and the abrupt phone calls that end as soon as I walk into the room. Even our sex life was perfunctory and without passion and soon even that dried up. I turned a blind eye to his affairs and ignored the pitying looks as I went about my business in the hospital we both worked. Now this.

Now everything's changed because he's leaving me for that empty airhead, fresh out of nursing college, Melissa Randall. I hate the very thought of her. Blonde, pretty and vacuous. Everything I despise because she reminds me I am well past my best and being replaced with a younger, more perfect version of what I used to be.

By the time I reach the intensive care suite, I feel sick to my stomach. Not of what I might find - no, Peter's heart attack couldn't have come at a better time. Maybe fate has lent me a helping hand because now he will be reminded of his own mortality.

The nurse on duty greets me with a worried frown and ushers me inside the room, saying kindly, "It looks worse than it is – you know that but he had a massive coronary and we are keeping him hooked up for his own good while we run some tests."

I nod and take a look at the man I married and feel – nothing. He looks pathetic where once he looked powerful and charismatic. His face is ashen and only the noise from the machine shows that he is still alive.

I manage to croak out, "What are his chances?"

"You'll have to see the doctor. He's doing his rounds at the moment but should be along soon." She hesitates and then says in a low voice, "I'm sorry, Alice. It must be a shock seeing him like this."

"Yes, it is a little." I half-smile and she gestures towards a seat by his bed. "Stay as long as you want."

Nodding, I take the seat and listen as the door clicks shut behind her.

It doesn't take long for Peter to wake up and as he blinks, mine is the first face he sees. I don't miss the resignation in his expression and know that I am the last person he wants here. However, I don't give

93

him that choice. I stay by his side with a stern expression and an unforgiving heart.

For the next four days, we talk and he tells me how it's going to be. Lily will be taken care of and he will always be a father to her but nothing has changed. He will be moving out and filing for divorce. I listen with a hardening heart as he blames me for the breakdown of our marriage. I steel myself for the future where he parades his 'girlfriends' in front of Lily until finally one of them becomes her stepmother. I hate the fact that he will no doubt flourish in his new life and will continue to enjoy the lifestyle that a doctor at the top of his game can enjoy and I despair as I think of my own future struggling to make ends meet bringing up a child on my own. Finally, it is the realisation that I will be on my own because any trust I ever had in men has long gone after what happened six months before Lily was born. I have struggled since that night which is why we are probably at this crossroads now.

However, the final nail in Peter's coffin came when he ordered me to leave and never come back. He wanted to see Melissa, not me. He never once asked after Lily, even though my mother was caring for her while I stayed by his bedside. He was more preoccupied with sending his lover texts while I sat by his bed and berating me for refusing to leave.

Any love that man had for me was replaced by a bitter, twisted, hatred. When he threatened to call the nurse to have me forcibly removed, I stood and

94

looked at him with a blank, cold, expression and said dully, "Goodbye Peter. May you rot in Hell."

I remember turning away, his bitter laughter ringing in my ears as it followed me out of the room.

That night, I returned.

That night, I was dressed in my nurses' uniform.

That night, I walked towards the intensive care unit with only one purpose in mind. Securing mine and Lily's future.

That night, I sold my soul to the Devil for a second time and any humanity I had inside was left at the door.

I walked into his room as he slept in the early hours of the morning. The darkened room provided the cover I needed as I held the pillow over his face. I watched with satisfaction when I saw his smug face for the last time as I lowered the pillow over it and held it down with all my strength. As Peter's body jerked beneath me, I relished the feeling. Peter would never leave me now. I would be spared the humiliation of a broken marriage and spared watching him carry on with other women in front of me on a daily basis. Most of all, Lily would be spared from living in a broken home. She wouldn't be pushed between two families and having to fit in with his life. She wouldn't have her faith destroyed in men before she even understood what that is and she would never know what a failure her own father was and how easily he gave up on her. We would move on with our lives without all the problems that go with a broken marriage and Lily would always have fond memories of a father who loved her - I would make sure of it.

I twist and turn in my sleep as the memory of what I did haunts me in my nightmares.

My dreams wake me as they always do and I look around at the dark shadows in an unfamiliar room. My heart is beating so fast and just for a moment I think I see him there, at the foot of my bed, looking at me with a face twisted in rage and hatred. I sob and scoot back against my pillows as I see him holding something I will never come to terms with. The baby in his arms is still and lifeless and Peter looks at me with judgement in his eyes. Will I ever be free of the ghosts that haunt me from past actions? Can I ever shed the image of what I did all those years ago? I already know the answer as I sob and turn my face into the soft, plump pillow, as I try to block out my guilt. This is a nightmare that will never end, which is another reason why I'm here in the first place. Because of what I did all those years ago and the repercussions that will haunt me to my dying day.

Sleep is not the welcome relief that innocence enjoys. Sleep is a dark form of torture where guilty minds go to pay for their sins.

Sleep draws you into blissful oblivion and then traps you in nightmares. Sleep is something to dread where you think about what you've done and live knowing that you will never be free of past mistakes.

It's hard to be brave when you're alone in the dark. It's hard to forget when you are forced to watch your past mistakes as if someone is playing them over and over and compelling you to watch. Only the light of dawn can chase them away, leaving me to disguise them in normality until they return at night. Will I ever be free, or will I spend the rest of my life trying to make sure my child never suffers as I did all those years ago? I would do anything to save Lily from what life considers acceptable. She deserves so much more, which is why I must see this through and keep her safe.

15

FLORENCE

"What do you think of her? She seems ok – nice, really."

David shrugs. "I think she's a little strange."

"You think everyone's strange."

He grins and holds out his arms and I walk into them secure in the knowledge that our future is now a bright one.

He leans down and whispers, "Shall we have an early night?"

Smiling against his chest, I think about how things have changed for us since we started delving into the secrets of sex therapy. Although Estelle is on her Christmas break, we wasted no time in researching ways to spice up our love life and subsequently our marriage. I never knew how much I missed sex with David until we started enjoying it again. However, now we have gone from once every so often to once a day and sometimes twice. It's all good fun but Alice's words are haunting me because she's planted a seed of doubt that makes me worry if David is becoming an addict. So, with that in mind, I shake my head. "Maybe we should cool it over Christmas while we have guests. It wouldn't feel right with everyone in the house."

Pulling back, I look at him anxiously. "You don't mind, do you?"

I note the disappointment on his face as he shrugs, "Ok, no problem."

Feeling a little bad, I say brightly, "Why don't we grab a hot chocolate and head off to bed and watch Netflix. It will be lovely just snuggling up together and waking up refreshed on Christmas Eve."

He nods and as I make the drinks, I feel a little better about things. Yes, it's only a few days after all and is the right thing to do.

Just before we head up, I poke my head around the door to the living room and laugh as I see Oliver and Lily wrapped in each other's arms watching a film. They look up and I say gently, "We're off to bed. I hope you find everything you need, Lily and have a good night's sleep. It's Christmas Eve tomorrow and we have a lot to do."

"Thank you, Mrs Buckland, you too."

Laughing, I shake my head. "Call me Florence, darling. I'm not David's mother."

She smiles and I leave them to it, once again pleased that Oliver has found such a nice girlfriend. Yes, I have a good feeling about Christmas now and an even better one about the year ahead.

Christmas Eve dawns and I feel excited as I wake beside David and relish that pre-Christmas feeling that always makes me happy. Everything is bought, wrapped and placed under the tree. The food is waiting to be eaten, and the house cleaned and made to look amazing.

However, the reason I'm most excited is that today, Toby comes home.

Thinking about my son, I feel a happiness that never diminishes. Both of my boys are my reason for living and the result of years of care and guidance. The fact I didn't have a daughter never bothered me. I love my boys and they have never disappointed me. Both are extremely kind, caring and good looking. They excel at their studies along with anything else they put their minds to. Unlike some of my friend's children, they are never in trouble and always call and keep me informed of what they are doing. I miss Toby because for most of the time he lives away. He never went to university because he decided he wanted to start working immediately. He was accepted as an apprentice in a graphic design company and they allow him time at college as part of his apprenticeship. Toby is happy, so I am happy but I miss him because he has to work in Leeds and took a bedsit near his place of work and only visits sporadically.

However, today he is coming home and I can't wait.

David groans as I sit up and reaches out to pull me down beside him. "Don't leave me."

Laughing, I push him away and slip on my satin mules and reach for my robe. "Down boy, I have a lot to do. It's Christmas Eve unless you've forgotten and we have guests. Now, I need to shower and change before making an amazing breakfast to start the day."

He groans and pulls the pillow over his head as I head to our ensuite.

I'm surprised to find Alice already up and dressed when I head into the kitchen and she smiles brightly. "Happy Christmas Eve, Florence."

"Oh, the same to you, Alice. Did you sleep well?"

I notice the shadows under her eyes and feel anxious that the bed was uncomfortable.

She shakes her head. "I don't sleep well I'm afraid. In fact, ever since Peter died my life has never really been the same."

Reaching for the kettle, I feel a pang of sympathy for the kind woman and say gently, "It must have been hard."

"It was – still is, really. I know it's been over ten years since he died but I still have nightmares."

I say nothing as she sighs heavily and fixes me with a sad look that makes me hold my breath. "You see, our marriage wasn't as happy as yours is. Unfortunately, Peter had many affairs and didn't disguise them."

I feel shocked and she nods. "Yes, it was difficult because he was a doctor at the same hospital I worked at. I was always the woman who walked surrounded by whispers. I used to see the sympathy in the eyes of my colleagues and the derision in the eyes of the women he cheated on me with. Peter was a good-looking man and the women he dallied with wanted to take my place and made no secret of it."

I whisper, "What did you do, I'm not sure I could have coped with that?"

"It was hard, I'm not going to lie. You see, Lily was small, and we had to juggle things to care for her. My mother helped a lot, and I only worked part-time but we both thought it would be best for me to keep working. I never really understood why until his death." She laughs bitterly. "When he died, I discovered that far from having provided for our future, Peter was in a great deal of debt. There was no life insurance because he neglected to pay the premiums. They repossessed the house because the mortgage was in arrears and any savings I had were used to pay for the funeral."

I feel shocked as she speaks and it must show on my face because she smiles. "Don't feel bad, Florence, we got through it and it just reinforced my opinion of the man. You see, Peter was a gambling addict. He may have earned a good salary, but he spent it just as quickly and was an addict much like I described. Gambling was his greatest addiction but cheating followed a close second. I doubt he was really interested in the women he cheated on me with because he soon got bored of them and moved onto the next one. The thrill was always in the chase for him and as soon as they became clingy or demanding, he used me and Lily as an excuse to break it off."

She sighs and takes the mug of tea I hand her gratefully and I say warmly, "Well, you've done a fantastic job with Lily. She's a credit to you and it's obvious you have brought her up well."

A hard look enters her eyes and she nods. "Yes, Lily is everything to me and I will let nothing hurt her. You must feel the same about your boys, Florence. A mother's love is the greatest form of love there is. We will do anything to keep them safe, even it means overstepping the boundaries from time to time. I don't know about you but I'd do anything to keep the shadows from her eyes and the thought of anyone harming her fills me with the greatest fear."

I feel slightly disconcerted as I see the hard look in her eyes but know I'm the same. My family is everything to me and if I thought something was threatening them, I would spring into action, no questions asked. Nodding, I feel an affinity with the woman who has had it so hard and smile sympathetically. "You're an amazing woman, Alice. It must have been incredibly hard for you and Lily is a credit to all your hard work."

She smiles warmly. "Anyway, it's Christmas and you don't want to hear my tales of doom and gloom. Now, is there anything I can do to help because I may be your guest but I'll not be an idle one."

Jumping up, I start pulling the ingredients from the fridge to make us all a cooked breakfast.

"Yes, thank you. It will be good to have someone to help me, I'm so used to doing everything myself I've forgotten what it's like."

"Don't the boys pull their weight then?"

"Goodness no. I suppose it's my fault because when I gave up my job to care for them, I did everything myself. It was my job, and I was keen to do it well. The trouble is, I've now raised two men who don't lift a finger. They expect to be waited on and wouldn't even know how to crack an egg."

I see the disapproval in her expression and feel a little guilty as she says somewhat harshly, "You could work now they are more independent, why don't you?"

I feel a prickle of annoyance at the cheek of her question and I suppose it's because I do feel guilty, I say quickly, "I've decided that after Christmas I will do just that. Look for a job to bring a little more meaning into my life. It's been so long though, I'm not really sure where to start looking."

I see a little spark of respect in Alice's eyes as she nods with approval. "Yes, I think that's a good idea. Maybe there will be something at the hospital that would suit you. I'll ask around if you want me to."

Unsure whether that's what I had in mind; I just smile gratefully. "Thanks, that's kind of you."

We are interrupted as Lily heads into the room and I note the light burn a little brighter in Alice's eyes as she says happily, "Morning, darling, did you sleep well?"

Heading across to kiss her mother, Lily smiles. "Yes, thank you, did you?"

"Darling, how could I not, the room was very comfortable."

As I make Lily a cup of tea, I have to hand it to Alice. She has just done exactly what I would have, papered over any cracks to keep up the pretence that all is well. There is no reason to cause concern and make Lily worry about her, what would that solve? I can see that Alice is a very special person because even though her life has been hard and obviously still is, she will do anything for Lily not to notice.

16

Christmas Eve is one of my favourite days of the year. Everything is prepared and ready for the big day tomorrow and we can usually sit back and just enjoy some family time knowing that I have catered for everything. Having guests makes it a little different and so I feel a little relieved when Oliver announces that he and Lily are heading out to do some last-minute shopping.

Alice says quickly, "I thought you had already bought everything, darling?"

Lily rolls her eyes and smiles fondly at Oliver. "I have but as usual, Oliver is falling behind."

He grins. "What can I say, I'm not prepared. I need to get a few things and Lily's coming along for the ride."

Alice says quickly, "Be careful out there, it's a busy time and there will be a lot of traffic on the roads and hordes of shoppers in the stores."

She looks disapproving which annoys me a little and I say quickly, "I'm sure they'll be fine. Maybe you should grab some lunch out, my treat."

Oliver nods and as I reach for my purse, I note the irritation in Alice's eyes and sigh inside, feeling like the worst mother in the world.

Yes, I spoil my children. Yes, I give them everything they want and yes, I clear up after them and don't expect them to lift a finger to help.

However, I want to do all of the above because, like Alice, I put my children first and even though we go about things differently the end result is the same - their happiness.

They don't hang around for long and Alice helps me prepare the vegetables for Christmas dinner tomorrow. As we work, we chat about the usual problems that mothers face.

It must be around 1 pm that I hear a key in the front door and my heart leaps. He's home.

Placing my peeler down, I say with excitement, "That must be Toby."

Quickly, I rush to the door and squeal as I see the welcome sight of my other son. He grins in that lopsided way he has and I run into his arms. As he holds me close, I feel emotional and breathe a sigh of relief that he's home again.

David appears and I move aside to let him hug his son and I swallow hard when I see the emotion in their eyes. "It's good to see you, son."

Toby grins and I can tell he's glad to be home. I can't remember the last time he was; it was probably for a week in the summer, so it's been a long time.

I don't want to waste a minute of the time we do have and drag him towards the kitchen. "Come and meet Alice. She's Oliver's girlfriend Lily's mother, do you remember I told you they were staying for Christmas?"

He looks resigned to meeting a complete stranger and as we enter the room, Alice looks up with interest. "Alice, allow me to introduce my son, Toby."

She smiles and holds out her hand, saying pleasantly, "I'm pleased to meet you."

He nods and returns the greeting and I say briskly, "Pull up a stool and I'll make you a cup of tea. You must be desperate after that long journey."

"Thanks, mum."

As he sits beside Alice, she says with interest, "I understand you're a graphic designer. That sounds interesting."

He shrugs. "It is but I'm just learning so I just get to do the donkey work."

"We all have to start somewhere." She laughs and I interrupt, "So, tell me, Toby, is there a lady in your life at the moment?"

Groaning, he grins and shakes his head. "No mum, no one special. I'll leave that to my brother. Where is he by the way?"

"Gone to town with Lily. You know, Toby, you'll love her, she's an angel."

Toby looks disinterested and I laugh to myself. He couldn't care less about Oliver's girlfriend and with a pang, I remember that he actually couldn't care less about his brother either. To say they have a difficult relationship is an understatement. Once again, the anxiety re-surfaces as it always does when the two of them are under the same roof and I wish for the umpteenth time that I had a solution for our problems.

David soon joins us and puffs, "What have you got in that bag, iron bars?"

Toby laughs. "Trainers mainly and lots and lots of dirty washing."

Smiling, I can't disguise the joy I feel at having my son home. The whole family is now together and we can relax and enjoy Christmas as a slightly extended family. There was another reason that I invited them other than getting to know Lily and her mother. It was to avoid another awkward Christmas trying to ignore the fact that my sons hate each other and my husband is torn. At least with strangers in the house, they will all have to be on their best behaviour which makes me relax more than if we were here alone.

After devouring a plate of sandwiches and three cups of tea, David and Toby head off for some male bonding to the cinema room upstairs and Alice says brightly, "What a lovely lad you have there, Florence. Tell me, how old is he because at face value he looks exactly the same age as Oliver?"

I feel a little uncomfortable because now is not the time to divulge our family drama, so I laugh nervously and say quickly, "Yes they are close in age. It was both a blessing and a curse when they were growing up. They used to fight a lot and you should have heard the shouting, from me mainly."

I don't give her a chance to repeat her question as I look at the clock and say quickly, "Goodness, we don't have long and I haven't even delivered the neighbour's gifts. If you'll excuse me, I

109

really should get them done, you don't mind, do you?"

She shakes her head and says kindly, "No, you do what you need to. I'll tidy up here and make the men a cup of tea and take it up."

"No need for that, they have everything they need in the room. If they want anything, they can help themselves. It's why we designed it that way to stop me from having to trawl upstairs waiting on them. Genius really."

She laughs and I feel a little bad for leaving her and point to a pile of magazines on the settee in the corner of the kitchen. "Why don't you fix yourself a drink and curl up with a magazine? You can watch a movie, or something else if you prefer. I won't be long."

Smiling apologetically, I leave her to it, feeling a little bad. I should have delivered these before they came but I completely forgot. As I said though, it won't take long and I brave myself to face Celia and what is sure to be endless comparisons between her Christmas and mine.

17

Celia's house is only a few doors away from ours and almost identical in appearance. Like me, she enjoys the finer things in life and her home reflects that. Absolutely everything is in place and she frowns upon a single blade of grass out of place which is why I struggle to keep up with her.

I pass the beautiful potted trees entwined with fairy lights to reach her front door. The fresh wreath that hangs proudly from it smells divine of orange and fir. Self-consciously I check my appearance in her gleaming window by the side of an equally clean front door and ring the bell, anticipating what's coming.

It doesn't take long, and she throws open her door and exclaims loudly, "Darling, how lovely. Come in and enjoy a festive tipple."

I struggle out of my boots before I go inside and leave them on the porch because the inside of Celia's home would frown on any speck of dust from my shoe. As I follow her into her immaculate kitchen, I enjoy the smells of Christmas that always give me a warm feeling inside. Spices mixed with festive scents attack my senses and leave me reeling. Soft music plays from hidden speakers, those old-fashioned Christmas tunes that evoke feelings of Christmas past and dear memories. The smell of mulled wine on the cooker makes me dizzy with longing and I watch as Blake smiles and winks as he ladles some into a glass with a handle and hands it to me.

Celia smiles, "Here you go. I'm guessing this is your first drink."

I try to ignore their sympathetic looks because yes, as hard it is, we don't have the same treats at home that they enjoy. Wistfully, I remember a time when a bottle of mulled wine sat simmering on my stove and we never gave it a second thought. Now I have to make do with non-alcoholic replacements and as nice as they are, they just aren't the same.

I hand over the designer wrapped gifts and Celia squeals her thanks. "Lovely, darling and so beautifully wrapped. Here, let me go and retrieve yours from under the tree."

She scurries off and Blakes rolls his eyes. "I'll never understand women. Why do you make all this work for yourselves? Celia's been planning presents, food, social events and the decorations since the summer. If I even put a Christmas card in the wrong place, my life isn't worth living. You should all just relax and slob out a bit."

I'm spared from answering as Celia staggers into the room under a weight of designer boxes and says shortly, "You love it all really, Blake. If I didn't put as much effort into every aspect of running this home, you included, you wouldn't be as content as you are."

Laughing, he heads across and nibbles her neck and she giggles making me feel a little uncomfortable. Batting him away, she says firmly, "Now go and collect the turkey as I instructed you to do an hour ago. Any more mulled wine and you'll be over the limit and Christmas will be ruined."

He laughs and heads off and she rolls her eyes.

"Goodness, that man will send me to an early grave one way or another."

She winks and I think how lucky she is. Celia really does have it all. Even her children are perfect. Alyssia goes to Oxford and is studying the classics and Hugo attends a private school nearby where he excels at rugby and plays for the county. They fully expect him to play professionally and have none of the worries we live with. Blake's business is doing well and Celia doesn't work due to the large inheritance her grandmother left, meaning they never have to worry about money again. I'm pretty sure I'd have a permanent smug look on my face if I had *her* life.

As I sip the forbidden drink, I feel a little guilty for doing so. I vowed to stay teetotal to support David and even though I know the boys drink, they never would in his company.

Celia interrupts my thoughts. "Tell me about your visitor, what was her name again?"

"Alice."

"Well then, what's she like?"

"I'm not sure, really. She seems very nice, keen to help, no bother, you know the sort but there is

113

something about her that makes me feel uncomfortable."

"Like what?" Celia looks interested, and that's not unusual. She loves to gossip, and this is right up her street. "Well, she seems a little forced and to be honest, I feel as if she's judging me and finding me lacking."

Snorting, Celia helps herself to more mulled wine before pushing a plate of mini mince pies towards me on a silver platter. "Bloody cheek. Who does she think she is?"

I know it shouldn't but it feels good to offload to Celia. She has been a friend for a long time and even though she has changed since I first knew her, she's still the same person underneath the façade.

"I can't put my finger on it but she seems dismissive of the fact I don't have a job and has made me doubt my relationship with David."

"What?"

"Well, the thing is, Celia, David and I have sort of reached a new level this last week or so. We have decided to spice things up a little because they've grown quite stale. I kind of mentioned it to Alice, and she told me I was playing a dangerous game because David is a man with an addictive personality and if I let him, he'll add um… sex… to his list. She told me when I couldn't satisfy him, he would look elsewhere."

Celia's face is a picture as she stares at me incredulously. Then she bursts out laughing and I can't help but follow. I think the tears run down our faces as we laugh so hard, I almost fall off my barstool and she chokes out, "She's just jealous. God, you lucky bitch, tell me everything so I can put the same spell on Blake."

Her words surprise me because this is where the whole thing started - after my coffee with him. Maybe I got it wrong and they aren't this super loved up couple enjoying a fulfilling sexual relationship.

She must sense my surprise because she sighs heavily. "Don't get me wrong, darling, we don't have a problem, it's just that, well, it's all become a little perfunctory. Nothing ever changes and we always follow the routine to the letter. There's no passion there anymore, just familiarity."

She lowers her voice. "Between me and you, I've been thinking about asking him to indulge in a spot of porn of an evening to see if it lights a different flame."

I stare at her in surprise and she shrugs. "I've got to do something."

Thinking about the intimate lingerie currently residing under her Christmas tree, I wonder if Blake has the same wish. "You know, Celia, you should do what we did and look into getting a sex therapist."

"A what?"

"A sex therapist." I giggle. "David looks after the books of one and I interrupted a cosy lunch they were sharing, a week before Christmas. I thought he was having an affair at first until he told me what she really was. Well, we're booked in to see her in the new year but in the meantime have been doing our research online. Maybe you should do the same."

Celia's eyes sparkle and she looks interested. "You know, I think we will. Thanks, darling. Anyway, how are things otherwise, is Toby home?"

I nod and she takes a long look and then says in a softer voice, "I hope it all goes well. You know, one day those boys will grow up and realise that what happened was nobody's fault but fate. That will happen you know, take my word for it."

Nodding, I pull on my coat and sigh. "I know, I'm sure you're right. They're good boys really but best enjoyed apart."

Rolling her eyes, she follows me to the door and hugs me warmly. "Happy Christmas and thanks for the presents and the tip. I'll let you know how it pans out."

As I leave my friend, I feel glad I came. Celia knows me so well and it has diffused a little of the tension that's been building since Alice and Lily arrived. Now Toby's here it has just added to it and I keep on telling myself it's only for two more days and then life can return to normal - whatever that is.

18

Oliver and I split up at the mall because he told me he needed privacy to get something important. As I wait for him in the coffee shop, I think about Christmas with his family. To be honest, I've been dreading it because of one thing – my mother. She's always been way overprotective and the older I got, the more I realised just how weird it is. None of my friend's mothers questioned their every move. Any boys or girls I brought home were given the third degree and if anybody upset me, God help them. I've lost count of the times my mother marched me into the principal's office and demanded a particular child be expelled for bullying. After a while, it had the desired effect and the other kids left me alone. The trouble is, they also didn't want to be my friend because of *her*.

I often wonder what it would have been like if my father hadn't died. I suppose I make allowances for her because it must be super hard bringing up a child on your own where the money is tight.

However, to me, she has always been there with a loving smile and a ready ear to listen to my problems and I've known no different.

I watch as Oliver makes his way inside the coffee shop. My heart lifts as I see him and smile as

I think of how sweet he is being. I don't miss the lustful stares of a group of girls sitting at a nearby table and feel smug as his eyes search for me and then burn right through me as he finds his target. His look is powerful. It draws you in and holds you prisoner. He strips any defence you have in place and ruins you for anyone else. Oliver Buckland is a player and a good one at that.

As he heads towards me, I can't help remembering a different look that he has perfected over the years and it's one I never want to be on the receiving end of. He can cut a girl down with just a flash from his eyes or a snarl from those perfect lips. The girl who held his attention for a few moments at the party obviously heard something she didn't like because I remember seeing the hurt flare in her eyes and the disgust on her face. I wonder what he said to her because, by the looks of things, it wasn't nice.

"Hey, babe,"

He drops a light kiss on my willing lips and smiles. "I don't know why you love shopping so much. It's a modern-day form of torture as far as I'm concerned."

Laughing, I point to the bags he has gripped in his hands. "It looks as if you've been successful. Anything for me in there?"

Winking, he taps his nose. "Wait until tomorrow."

The shop is filling up, and it's becoming uncomfortable so he says with some irritation.

118

"Come on, let's find somewhere quieter and grab some lunch. It will keep us out of the house for a little longer."

As we walk, I think about what he said. Yes, it is a little stifling in his house and I say with concern, "Tell me what to expect. You said your brother arrives today, what's he like?"

I don't miss the hard edge creep into Oliver's eyes as his lips tighten and he snaps, "I can't stand him. You know most people think it would be good to have a brother but they haven't met mine. I've never met anyone so cold, rude and downright annoying."

"Why, isn't that what brothers do?"

I feel a pang because I would give anything to have a brother – or sister. Being an only child was very lonely growing up, making me determined to have a large family of my own one day.

He shakes his head. "It's annoying. I would give anything to be an only child. You know, I can't ever remember a time when we were that happy family you see on the television. Toby was always like a dark cloud on the horizon and dad was going through his own private hell, so we all had to tiptoe around him and try not to cause him any more problems."

Slipping my hand in his, I say softly, "Do you want to talk about it – your dad's problems, I mean?"

I watch the shutters come down as he sighs. "Not really. It's Christmas and should be a time for enjoying the moment. Dad's problems have always been there, and we have learned to live with them. They've become part of the family and we just occasionally dust them off before placing them back where they were, like an old piece of furniture we can't bear to get rid of. No, the sooner I leave home, the better. I can't wait to leave them all behind and start again."

I feel a little shocked because, on face value, Oliver's life is a dream. Although, like me, he appears eager to leave home and I say with interest, "What are you going to do when you graduate?"

He grips my hand a little tighter and says with determination, "I will move somewhere far away from here and make sure I get a good job. I want you to come with me and we can rent a house together and start living our best lives."

Feeling a little overwhelmed, I laugh nervously, "Don't I have a say in this? I mean, what if my plans are different?"

Stopping suddenly, he spins around and I feel the heat travel through my body as I see the dark look enter his eyes. He pulls me tightly against him and growls, "You will always be by my side, Lily Adams because it was written in the stars. You and me, together for eternity and that's why I'm keen to move on. I knew as soon as I saw you, we were meant to be together. Don't ask me how, it was just a bolt of something amazing that hit me where it counted."

His eyes soften and he leans down, claiming my lips in a soft, sweet kiss and I melt against him. "I love you little Lily flower and we will have an amazing life together."

I shrug off the warning bells going off in my head.

I shrug off the fact I obviously don't have a say in the matter and I shrug off the doubts that have appeared like cracks in the wall of a newly built house. He's right, Oliver and Lily *were* meant to be together. There's an invisible chord that binds us and keeps us tethered in a raging storm. That bond will never break because we are stronger – together.

Maybe that's why my mother doesn't like him because I can see in her eyes the truth about how she feels. For some reason, she doesn't approve of him and I wonder what she can see that I am blinded to.

However, it's Christmas and the happiest time of the year and as we head happily towards our favourite restaurant, I leave any doubts I have for the future in the past where they belong.

19

"Oh God, he's here already. Prepare yourself."

We pull up behind a sleek sports car on the drive and I say with surprise, "Goodness, is he rich or something, that car is impressive?"

"No, just incredibly spoilt."

"And you're not I suppose."

He grins because we both know that Oliver's car cost a small fortune and he is certainly not one to talk.

"No, of course, you're right but Toby has always been the favourite. They tiptoe around him and always go above and beyond the norm which is probably why I resent him so much."

"That's not his fault though." I look at Oliver who appears tense and on edge and he snaps, "Maybe not but what *is* his fault is that he's a complete and utter bastard. Don't be sucked into his obvious charm offensive when you meet him, Lily, because I've never met anyone as devious as he is."

I feel a little nervous as I follow Oliver into the house, wondering what sort of monster is waiting inside.

However, as we walk into the bright, inviting kitchen, I see a man around the same age as Oliver laughing at something Florence is saying, and it strikes me how normal he appears. He certainly doesn't look like the monster that Oliver speaks of and as he looks up and our eyes meet, I see the interest in his as Florence says, "Oliver, look who's home."

Oliver nods and says reluctantly, "Good to see you, bro."

Toby raises an eyebrow. "Is it?"

Florence giggles nervously and I see her share a look with my mother who is looking at the scene with interest. She catches my eye and smiles softly and yet I see a hard edge to her that I know means she disapproves of something.

Oliver appears to withdraw into himself as his brother nods in my direction. "You must be Lily. May I offer you my commiserations for being saddled with Oliver. Word of advice, get out now while you still can."

He smiles to take the heat from his words and Florence rolls her eyes and says quickly, "Honestly, they've been together for two minutes and are already bickering. Now, let me make you all a nice cup of tea and roll out the Christmas cake. We may as well start eating our way through the mountain of food cluttering up my cupboards."

Oliver drags me over to the couch in the corner of the room and whispers, "You see what he's like. A total idiot. We should keep our distance because it will only end in a fight if I allow him to get to me."

I feel nervous as I perch on the seat beside him because I feel uncomfortable about the way Toby's eyes followed us as we walked away. He looks very different from Oliver. Where Oliver is fair, Toby is dark. His hair, his eyes and his complexion. I wonder who he takes after because he looks nothing like Florence or David. Come to mention it, neither does Oliver which strikes me as a little odd. Both of them are like chalk and cheese and I wonder what the true story is here because it's becoming increasingly obvious there's a secret this family is holding onto tightly and whatever it is, it's breaking them apart.

After a while, Oliver and I make our excuses and head off to the cinema room for some privacy. I'm glad to distance myself from the obvious tension in the room and sink down onto the soft couch and groan with relief. "That feels good."

Oliver grins wickedly, "I can make you feel even better if I lock the door."

Feeling a little panicked at the thought of being caught in a compromising position with Oliver, I shake my head quickly. "Absolutely not. What if my mother tries to get in, or yours? No, we must be good for two days at least because you wouldn't want to be on the receiving end of my mother when she's angry."

Flicking on the large television set, Oliver wraps his arm around my shoulders and pulls me tightly against him, whispering, "Then we'll just have to curl up here instead. You know, Lily, I'm not sure if this was such a good idea."

"What?" I feel a prickle of alarm as I wonder what he means. Is he referring to the situation, or us as a couple?

He groans and places his feet on the table in front of us. "Spending Christmas together. I mean, I want you to like me, not be put off by my family."

Staring at him in surprise, I say incredulously, "Of course I'm not put off you."

He raises his eyes. "Are you sure about that? I mean, you seem a little distant if I'm honest."

"What do you mean?"

He stares at me with a cold look and a spark of fear grips hold of my better judgement. "I don't know, you appear to have withdrawn a little, and this is just advertising it."

"What is?"

He seems annoyed and snaps, "You, pulling away from me. Two days ago, you wouldn't hesitate. You wouldn't care about what other people think and just want to be as close to me as possible, as I do you."

He shakes his head. "Now you are making excuses and it bothers me. Maybe you're having doubts and that worries me."

I feel alarmed as I see the hurt in his eyes. I never thought he'd be hurt by my refusal over something so small. However, I can see that Oliver is struggling with being here and feel a little bad that I'm not supporting him when he needs me the most, so I say quickly, "Lock the door, Oliver."

125

A wicked grin appears on his face, as he springs to his feet and locks the door. Then he increases the volume on the television until the sound of gunfire is crackling around the room. As he unfastens his belt, he walks towards me with so much heat in his gaze, I swallow hard. Then I lift my top above my head and unfasten my bra and look at him with the same heated look. I can't help it; I want him with a hunger that never appears to be satisfied.

As Oliver pulls me roughly against him, any reservations I had fall into a puddle of desire at my feet. Then as Oliver makes love to me it feels different. There's a desperation, an urgency to him, that raises things to a different level. Maybe it's because he's so stressed, or maybe it's the excitement of knowing our families are not far away but this time sex with Oliver is more intense and as we lay panting on the floor afterwards, I'm not sure I'm ok with what just happened. If I had to put a label on my feelings, I am startled to discover I feel used and a little betrayed.

However, Oliver appears in a much better mood and I'm glad he's not as edgy. It's obvious his family is divided and maybe he just needs a little more attention than normal. Perhaps I should just try and make him happy because it must be hard spending time with someone you don't get on with and all he needs is a little more reassurance than usual.

As we settle down to watch the film, I make every excuse in the world for him rather than face

what is growing by the hour – the realisation that
I've just made a terrible mistake.

20

Once the film finishes, Oliver appears in a better mood and we head down and join the rest of the family. My mother looks up and I see the hardness enter her eyes as she sees Oliver's hand in mine.

Dropping it quickly, I head across and say lightly, "Are you having a good time, mum? Sorry, I don't feel as if I've seen much of you today."

"Yes, darling, I'm having a lovely time, thank you. So, tell me, how was shopping?"

"Great thanks, although it's hard battling the last-minute crowds on Christmas Eve, I don't think I'll ever get used to that."

Florence interrupts, "I avoid it like the plague. I suppose I've got that luxury because when you don't work you can be more organised than most."

She looks at mum and smiles sympathetically. "I understand you're a nurse, Alice. It must be particularly busy for you; I'm in awe that you manage to cope with Christmas at all."

Mum shrugs. "I don't know any other way, to be honest. I've always had to plan for things and be one step ahead at all times. If I let my standards slip, then chaos would reign instead."

I grin and nod my head vigorously. "If there's one characteristic I want to share with my mum, is her super organising skills. She is second to none and I'm in awe of how she keeps everything running so smoothly."

Mum laughs. "Only one of my skills, darling. I hope you inherit a lot more than that."

She smiles and I ache to move across and curl up on her lap as I did as a child. I long to feel her stroke my hair and kiss the top of my head telling me that everything will be ok. I want to believe in the fairy tale and happy ever after but my rose-coloured future is turning a distinct shade of grey. I'm not sure when it all started to go wrong but as Oliver laughs at something his father says, it strikes me it started when I met him.

Feeling a little uneasy about how quickly this seed of doubt is sprouting roots, I turn my attention back to the women and watch Florence making some festive looking drinks.

"They look amazing, what's in them?"

She laughs happily. "Cranberry fizz with orange juice and blood-red orange slices to decorate. I always put a sugar crust on the rim of the glass and pop in a straw to make it look more festive. Here, try one and see what you think."

She passes me one and as I take a sip, the bubbles tickle my tongue and the sweet taste contrasts with the sharpness of the orange. "Wow, that's amazing."

She grins. "I'm glad you like it. Maybe you could hand them out to the others."

Mum says quickly, "I'll give you a hand."

Florence turns away and sets about filling some bowls with crisps and nuts and I head across to

David and Toby. Handing them each a glass, I say shyly, "Compliments of Florence."

David smiles warmly, "Thanks, Lily. Have you met my son, Toby?"

I can feel Oliver staring at me from his position on the other side of his father and feel myself blush as I nod, "I'm pleased to meet you."

He takes the glass from my hand and as he does, his fingers brush against mine causing me to nearly drop the glass. He smiles sweetly and says softly, "Thanks, babe."

I notice the irritation on Oliver's face that is quickly disguised as my mother hands him a drink and sets a bowl of nuts down on the table in front of them. Glad of the distraction, I quickly head back to grab my own and am glad when mum joins me and whispers, "Are you ok, darling? You seem a little out of sorts."

Battling the tears away, I say as brightly as I can, "I'm just tired, I guess. Christmas always does that to me. I work so hard in the weeks up to it, when I relax it takes its toll."

Florence hears and nods her head in agreement. "I'm the same, Lily. It's such a whirlwind in the run-up to Christmas, it's almost a relief when you can relax but then my body gives out on me. Maybe we should both put our feet up and take it easy."

Mum nods before saying with interest. "Do you go to church at all over Christmas?"

David laughs from his comfortable position on the sofa. "You've got to be joking, Alice. It would take a crowbar to prise us out of here on Christmas Eve, and Christmas Day. No, we're all nicely positioned for two days of eating too much and overindulging in every way."

He winks at Florence who colours up a little and says quickly, "Take no notice of him, why, did you want to go?"

Mum nods. "Lily and I always attend midnight mass. It's our family tradition and I'm keen to keep at least one of them going."

Florence nods. "Then we'll all go."

The men groan and she says with determination. "Enough of that, we have guests and we must be mindful they have needs. It will be fun, anyway and quite frankly, long overdue."

She glares at her family and I try not to laugh because the men look far from happy at the thought of being dragged to the church in the early hours.

As the afternoon turns to evening, I've lost count of the number of brightly coloured cocktails that Florence makes with such style. It's good fun as we all chill in the brightly lit kitchen and I feel glad we came. Usually, it's just mum and I sitting in the flat sharing a lonely Christmas for two. There are none of the comforts that this family take for granted and we spend much of it watching Christmas movies and playing board games. As I hear the teasing and loud conversation around me, I realise what I've been missing out on all these years. Glancing across at my mother, I see her laughing at something Florence is telling her and feel happy for her. She

131

doesn't laugh much and, come to think of it, doesn't have many friends. It never seemed to matter because she was always so busy and when she was home cared for me.

However, faced with the fact my own life is moving on, I worry about her. Thinking of her in the lonely flat on her own fills me with fear because her whole life has revolved around me at the centre of it. I wonder how she will cope when I move on and have my own home? Then again, I wonder how I will cope because it's a scary world out there without her by my side to look out for me.

Loud cheers take my attention and I notice Oliver shouting at something on the television and Florence says, "Calm down, Oliver, why are you being so loud?"

He looks up and I note the brightness in his eyes as he sneers, "What, can't I even raise my voice in my own home?"

I watch Florence and David share a look and David says softly, "Don't be rude to your mother, Oliver."

Oliver sneers. "Why, in case I tarnish the image of perfection she's created to disguise the rot in our family."

"Oliver!"

David yells loudly and I watch in horror as Oliver rolls of the settee and walks towards me, looking a little unsteady. Toby looks angry and grabs his arm and steers him towards the door. I can't hear what he says to him but whatever it is it causes him to pull away roughly. "Shut the fuck up, you don't get to tell me what to do."

David jumps to his feet and Florence cries out, "Stop it, all of you."

I feel shocked and as I catch my mother's eye, she shakes her head in disapproval. As I swing my gaze back towards Oliver, I see David and Toby frogmarch him from the room as Florence says awkwardly, "I'm so sorry, I don't know what came over him. Anyway, if you'll excuse me, I'll see if they need any help."

Silence now fills the room where just a few moments ago it was filled with anger. Mum looks at me and says in a slightly shocked voice, "I thought they didn't drink."

"What do you mean, they don't?"

She lowers her voice and whispers, "Well, somebody obviously didn't tell Oliver that. He looks smashed."

I stare at her in shock and shake my head. "You're wrong, Oliver hasn't touched a drop all day."

"Are you sure about that, darling? I mean, I know when I see someone who is under the influence. If it's not alcohol, it must be drugs."

"NO!" I shout the answer as if I'm telling myself more than her. "No, Oliver doesn't do drugs, I would know if he did."

"Are you sure about that, darling?"

My head spins as I try to take in what's just happened and say weakly, "He doesn't."

Mum takes my hand in hers and squeezes it tightly. "You know, Lily, I'm sure he could lay his hands on all sorts of things at Uni. Are you telling me he's never been offered them? I'm sure outside of the home he enjoys a drink as well. I'm not that naïve, I know what goes on in a university besides studying, I'm not stupid."

She looks at me with an intensity that offers no place to hide and I say with a slight edge to my voice, "Yes, he drinks. We all do but he hasn't today. As for drugs, yes, it goes on but we don't indulge, we never have. Oliver would be a fool to because his whole position on the football team hinges on him being clean and drug-free. They have regular testing, so it just isn't worth it."

Mum looks thoughtful. "Do you think he's agitated because of his brother?"

"Who, Toby?"

"Unless he has another one, of course, Toby."

"Maybe, but why fly off the handle so quickly over nothing, it doesn't make sense?"

Mum sighs heavily. "Nothing much does. Maybe he just needs a lie-down and to relax a little. I'm sure everything will be fine."

We are interrupted as Florence returns looking a little shaken. "I'm sorry, Alice but I think there's something wrong with Oliver. He looks as white as a sheet and is babbling. I'm sorry to ask but do you think you could take a look at him?"

I make to go with her and mum says firmly, "Stay here, darling, I'll take a look and you can see him when he feels a little better. I'm sure it's nothing."

As she heads off with Florence, the door opens almost as soon as they leave and Toby enters looking so angry, I can almost taste it.

I look up anxiously and he shakes his head. "Save your worry for someone who deserves it, Lily. That pathetic excuse of a brother of mine is raging drunk and I can never forgive him for that."

"What?!"

I stare at him in shock and he sets a small silver flask of alcohol down on the table and says sadly, "I found this under his bed. It's almost empty and by the looks of it, is now inside his system. He's a bastard because he knows we can't have even a sniff of it in the house. He's lucky he's out cold because otherwise I'd send him to oblivion myself."

"But I've been with him all day and he hasn't touched a drop; it makes little sense."

Toby shrugs and handles the flask carefully. "I've lived with an addict long enough to know they are extremely good at hiding their addiction. Just because you didn't see him drink, it doesn't mean anything. Tell me, was he with you every minute of the day?"

My face falls, and he laughs, "I thought not."

Suddenly, his face softens, and he draws near and whispers, "Word of warning, get out now while you still can. Oliver has a lot of problems and you don't want to get caught up in them. You seem a lovely girl and take this as it's meant. Another

135

human being looking out for another because if you continue with him, he will drag you down to his level and ruin your life. Trust me, I've been there."

We hear footsteps and Toby tucks the flask in his pocket and says urgently, "I have to dispose of this, we can't have it in the house. Listen, if you need to talk, I'm here. Just be careful, Lily, promise me that at least."

He heads towards the back door as Florence enters the room looking tearful and shaken. She sees the fear in my expression and sighs heavily. "He's asleep, at least that's what your mother says. David is so angry he's had to work it off in the gym in the garage. I can't tell you how disappointed we are in Oliver."

She must see my confused expression because she says softly, "I'm sorry, Lily, there are a lot of things you don't know about and now is not the time to drag them up. Oliver knows we don't tolerate drinking in this house and yet has done so, anyway. Your mother has assured me that's all it is and I'm thankful for that at least."

She sits on the settee and puts her head in her hands and sobs, leaving me feeling uncomfortable and unsure what to do. The only thing I can think of is to grab a tissue and sit beside her and as she takes it, she says gratefully, "I'm sorry. You must wonder what on earth is going on? You see, the thing is, our family ties are close to breaking point and I'm doing everything I can to keep that from happening.

Oliver and Toby have never got along and David has his own set of problems to deal with."

I smile weakly, "If it's any help Oliver is fine at Uni. He's popular, well-liked and has many friends. He doesn't drink too much and definitely doesn't do drugs. He's a model student and you should be proud of him. I'm not sure why he's done this but if he has, it's completely out of character."

She looks up sharply, "What do you mean *if* he has done this? Of course, he has."

I'm not sure whether to voice the doubts in my head, so I just smile. "Yes, of course. You know, maybe he ate something when we were out at lunch. Possibly the food didn't agree with him and this is his reaction to it."

Florence sighs and shakes her head sadly. "That's sweet of you but I'm not stupid. I know when someone is drunk, and that's exactly what he is. How he came to be is a mystery that doesn't really matter because just the fact he is disappoints me on so many levels. Anyway, I should head out to the garage and check on David. He is fragile around the subject and it will have affected him. Help yourself to whatever you like, I won't be long."

She leaves me feeling anxious, disbelieving and unsure about anything and everything. I'm not sure what to think but as Toby returns, I look up and he smiles sweetly. "Come on, let's get out of here."

"What do you mean?"

The look he gives me tells me to stay exactly where I am because it promises to open a rabbit hole I should avoid at all costs. However, something is compelling me to walk towards it and jump because as he stretches out his hand to pull me up, I find myself grasping it and as our skin makes contact for the second time, a warning siren sounds loudly in my head. I am in so much trouble.

21

Toby's car is much like the man himself, rich, gorgeous and super cool. It's powerful, smooth and the subject of many admiring looks as we speed through the streets that now have a smattering of freshly fallen snow, covering them in a magical, winter blanket.

Toby turns the stereo on high and haunting Christmas songs fill the car as we head off into the unknown.

After a while, he turns the music down and sighs heavily. "I'm sorry, Lily. I had to get out of there, which for me was quite a record."

"A record?"

He grins. "Yes, I lasted exactly one-hour longer than I usually do and I think I know why."

He looks sideways at me and grins. "And I'm looking at her."

I feel my face flush and he laughs. "Don't tell me you didn't notice the attraction. I could tell it a mile off."

I feel angry and snap. "I'm not attracted to you." Shrugging, he changes gear and says softly, "That's not what I'm talking about. I'm talking about my attraction to *you*."

His words knock the breath from my body as I struggle to breathe. I'm not sure what to say and he laughs. "I've shocked you – good."

"Why is that good?"

"Because now you know. It's not just because you're with my brother either."

"What do you mean by that?"

"Well, it was quite a game we played. He would hit on my girlfriends and I'd do the same to him. Sometimes it worked but often didn't. I'm sorry, old habits and everything."

I'm not sure whether to feel angry or flattered and say tightly, "I think you should take me back."

Laughing, he pulls the car to a stop and leans across, his arm resting on the backrest of my seat and lifts his finger to my chin. Tilting it up, I can feel his hot breath on my face as his eyes penetrate mine, making my mind empty as I think of nothing but the fact that I want to feel those lips on mine. It feels forbidden, wrong and yet so exciting. Leaning towards me, he whispers, "I could kiss you right now and you would want every tantalising taste of it. You would crave it and like a drug want more."

I battle my own stupid weakness and swallow hard. "You're wrong, I love Oliver – your brother."

He strokes my cheek. "I'll remind you of that when you're in my bed."

Batting his hand away, I take a few deep breaths and say angrily, "Take me home."

Pulling back, he suddenly changes before my eyes and looks broken and defeated. Reaching behind me, he pulls a bunch of flowers as if from nowhere and says sadly, "As soon as I've said 'hi' to my parents."

Blinking at the sudden change in atmosphere, I look around and with a pang see we have stopped at a cemetery. He shrugs and I see the tears glisten in his eyes as he smiles. "Come, I'll introduce you."

My earlier anger and indignation evaporate in a heartbeat as I scramble from the car and pull my coat around me tightly to protect me from the snow that is falling faster.

Toby grabs the flowers and indicates a grave nestling among some trees, seemingly on its own in the corner of the churchyard.

As I follow him, I wonder what I'm about to discover and yet know what it's like to visit a parent's grave.

We draw close and I see the white marble headstone, gleaming as cleanly as one of Florence's pans as Toby lays the flowers on the grave that reads,

RYAN AND ANGELA BUCKLAND.
LOVING PARENTS OF TOBY AND TAKEN
FAR TOO SOON.
Be still. Close your eyes. Breathe.
Listen for my footfall in your heart.
I am not gone but merely walk within you.

"That's beautiful."

Toby nods. "It's a quote by Nicholas Evans. Florence found it for me and it kind of works."

I watch as a lone tear escapes and take his hand in mine and squeeze it, before saying softly, "It hurts doesn't it?"

He nods and I say in a whisper. "I never really knew my father. I have a few memories of him but they are becoming blurred with time."

"You're lucky, I never knew mine."

His words shock me and he pulls me a little closer. "They died when I was just a few months old. A car accident - at least it was quick I suppose."

I say nothing and he says in a small voice, "They left me with my grandparents which was a blessing because their car burst into flames when a tanker lost control on the motorway."

I'm not sure what to say, so just whisper, "My father died of a heart attack. My mother speaks of him and how amazing he was. A brilliant doctor and a loving husband and father. Apparently, he was devoted to us and I was the apple of his eye – her words, not mine."

I smile and Toby smiles with me. "You're very lucky."

I shiver and he reaches out and pulls me against him to offer warmth, nothing more and we stand looking at his parent's grave as the flakes of snow settle on the bright red flowers he brought them. We stand in silence, both of us remembering our parents who can no longer stand beside us and no longer share in our lives and enjoy the things that so many people take for granted. We have been cheated of the one thing every child deserves to experience, a loving family with parents who shape their path in the future. However, Toby and I now share a bond that is strengthening whatever this is that's growing between us, so I say in a small voice, "Thank you."

"For what?"

"For allowing me to share this moment with you."

He pulls me tighter and says gently, "I knew you'd understand. Florence and David are my parents and always have been. They raised me as their own and I know they love me as much as Oliver, sometimes even more."

"Why do you say that?" His words surprise me and he shrugs. "I'm not sure why but Dad has always been particularly close to me. You see, my father was his brother, and they were inseparable. Maybe he sees a little of my father in me and it brings him back. I've always had a good relationship with him which is why Oliver is jealous. I don't blame him really, I mean, if I were in his shoes, I'd be the same. After all, he is their blood and real son. He deserves to come first, it's the law."

"Nonsense."

He looks at me in surprise and I shake my head. "Just because they didn't create you, you are still family. Anybody can create a life but it takes someone pretty amazing to shape it. Your parents have given Florence and David the most precious gift and how you've grown up is a credit to them.

They have taught you values that you live by. They have been there to dry your tears and provide a loving home. They have guided you through childhood and are what makes people into parents. You are just as much their child as Oliver and he should just be happy to have a brother because quite frankly, it sucks being an only child."

I break off as I feel the bitter tears fall that are never far away. I feel so lonely and it's not because my mother doesn't love me. If anything, she loves me too much and sometimes it's stifling.

Toby pulls me around to face him and wipes my tears away. He smiles sweetly. "Don't be lonely, Lily. You are beautiful, sweet and kind. People like you will never be lonely because ultimately, you're the type of person who attracts people to them. You may have had a painful start but at least you have your mum who adores you, it's obvious. It's no wonder my brother fell for you because apparently it's easy to."

I feel a little self-conscious as he lowers his lips to mine and this time I wait for the contact. I know it's so wrong of me and yet I go there anyway because moments like this don't come along often, sometimes they never do. Then as I taste Toby's lips, I taste hope, a new direction and the feeling that I've been rescued.

22

We are reluctant to leave but know that we must.

As we head for home it doesn't feel awkward between us. It feels like the most natural feeling in the world and I wonder what that will mean for my relationship with Oliver.

Whatever happens next, I wouldn't change anything that just happened. Even if we never talk again, we have shared something so special I will treasure the memory forever.

We pull up on the driveway and Toby's hand finds mine and squeezes it hard. "Thanks, Lily. Don't worry about the next couple of days, I won't ruin Christmas for everyone. I'm here for you and when you're ready, maybe look me up and we can see if this is as special as I think it could be."

He doesn't wait for an answer and just exits the car, leaving me to scramble after him and I wonder what will happen. How will I feel when I see Oliver and will the guilt pull me under?

As soon as we head inside, mum meets us in the hallway looking anxious. "Where have you been?"

I feel worried and say quickly, "Oh no, is Oliver ok?"

She nods and I don't miss the calculating look she gives us. Toby smiles sweetly. "I thought Lily could use a distraction. I hope we didn't worry you."

145

He turns to me and says airily, "Thanks for your help, Lily. It was good to have company."

He leaves us to it and mum says, "Well?"

For some strange reason, I don't want to share Toby's secret with anyone, even her. Maybe it's because it feels so intimate to have something between us, so I just shrug. "He wanted to get something for Florence and needed my help."

"Where is it then?"

Blushing, I realise we have no parcel or anything, so I say hastily. "It's in his car. Anyway, how is Oliver, can I see him now?"

Rolling her eyes, she says shortly, "If you like. Though, I must say, that young man has a lot to answer for. How could he be so cruel as to drink in front of his father? I'll never understand the thoughtlessness of some people."

I let her rant on about Oliver as we walk towards his room because I'm grateful for the distraction. Maybe she's right to disapprove of him and I should have listened to her in the first place. I knew she didn't approve of him and I couldn't see why. Now it's becoming more obvious that we are growing apart and I'm not sure what to do about it.

Luckily, mum leaves me to check on Oliver and I feel nervous as I creep into his darkened room. I make out a figure huddled under the bedclothes and hear him groan. As I approach the bed, I wonder if the guilt will show on my face and as he turns to me, I say gently, "Are you ok?"

He groans again. "I must have eaten something because I feel so sick. They think I was drunk but you know I've had no alcohol but they don't believe me."

Sitting beside him, I nod sympathetically. "I told them."

He looks so vulnerable my heart breaks under the guilt weighing it down and I feel foolish for what happened earlier with Toby. He smiles weakly. "At least you still love me."

I feel my heart thumping. "Of course, I do."

Reaching out, he entwines his fingers with mine and says gruffly. "I can't wait to get back to Uni. At least we can be ourselves and not worry about anyone else. Nobody judges us there and I don't have to deal with my brother."

At the mention of Toby, I feel the heat race through me and wonder if the guilt shows on my face. However, Oliver doesn't appear to notice it and almost spits, "It wouldn't surprise me if he spiked my drink. It's just the kind of thing he would do."

"What? Why would he do that?"

I try not to think about the fact he was the one who found the hip flask under Oliver's bed and after what happened next; I start to feel as if there might be some truth to Oliver's words.

He says sadly, "Because he hates me."

I think I hold my breath. "Why?"

"He always has. I think he resents my relationship with my parents."

I say nothing and just allow him to talk and he sighs heavily. "Lily, Toby isn't my brother by birth, just circumstance."

Feeling bad that I already know and from his hated brother at that, I stay silent and just smile reassuringly.

"I shouldn't say anything but he's really my cousin. I never knew my Aunt and Uncle because they died…"

He breaks off and takes a deep breath. "The day I was born."

I stare at him in shock and he nods. "They were coming to see me at the hospital when a tanker hit their car on the motorway. They never stood a chance, and that's why Toby hates me so much."

"But that's ridiculous, it's not your fault."

"To him it is because if I hadn't been born on that day, they wouldn't have been on the road at the time of the accident. He was left in the care of his grandparents and after the shock, it was decided that he come and live with us. However, he grew up knowing the story and as he grew, so did his resentment towards me."

"Oliver, that's ridiculous, even you must see you're not to blame."

Reaching out, Oliver pulls me close and I feel bad as he says gently, "It hit dad the hardest. He adored his brother, and they were close. It's why he started to drink. He just couldn't deal with what happened and felt so incredibly guilty. Mum had two young babies to care for and he was unravelling fast. It's a credit to her we're all still here because I know she struggled with the whole situation."

"Poor Florence and your poor father. How long was he an alcoholic?"

"He still is."

I stare at him in shock and he smiles sadly. "You never get over it. That's why we have no alcohol in the house. The temptation would be too great, so we avoid it. I can't believe they thought I was drinking; I would never do that knowingly."

"And you think your brother is responsible?"

He nods. "It can be the only explanation. Maybe he spiked the drinks my mum gave us. I can't think of anything else it could be."

He looks so upset I feel like the biggest bitch in the world. Suddenly, I'm torn between two brothers because I believe Oliver. I've been with him all day and know he didn't drink willingly. Then there's Toby and the flask he disposed of. Was it him? Did he spike Oliver's drink to make him look bad in front of us all? Why did he target me, was it just to get back at his brother? Suddenly, I feel like a grade-A fool and the tears threaten to give away my guilt as I figure he has used me as a pawn in a bitter game of revenge.

Oliver pulls my head down onto his chest and strokes my hair. "At least I have you, Lily flower. You are the only person in my life who I can trust. You are pure, innocent and all mine. Our future is bright because nothing will ever come between us. I'll make sure of it."

As I lie on Oliver's chest, I feel my heart breaking. What have I done? I've been dragged into a situation that spans years of blame and revenge and now I've played right into Toby's hands. I feel like such a fool and vow to stand by Oliver despite what happens next because I believe him. Ultimately, I know him better than anyone and he isn't this person they want me to believe he is. My heart hardens against Toby because now I can see clearly. As soon as he arrived, everything started to unravel, and I have played right into his hands. Thank God I found out before it was too late.

23

FLORENCE

I feel so angry at Oliver. How could he do that; he knows how dangerous it is? I find David in the garage punishing himself on the running machine and wait for him to calm down. We had the garage converted into a gym because that's David's coping mechanism – fitness. He replaced drinking with it and until now hasn't had to use the escape much but now I'm glad he has it.

As he slows down, I hand him a towel. "I'm sorry that happened."

Shrugging, he wipes his neck and face and shrugs. "It was nothing new, the bickering, I mean. What was new though was the alcohol. What's Oliver playing at?"

I shake my head sadly. "I don't know. To be honest, I thought having a girlfriend would have calmed him down a little. It's why I invited them. Lily is such a nice girl, I thought she could keep him under control."

David looks worried. "What if it happens again?"

I try not to face the biggest fear I have this Christmas and smile reassuringly. "It won't. I think this is a wake-up call for him. He knows the consequences if he loses it. No more chances and cut off with no inheritance, that was what we agreed – right?"

We stare at each other, neither one of us really believing what we agreed. Oliver has always been challenging and prone to violent rages when challenged. Toby has often borne the brunt of them because for some reason, he just can't stop winding him up. It's become a cat-and-mouse game with them and I am keen to diffuse the situation that is obviously building.

David steps off the machine and sighs. "Listen, we can't dwell on it because it's Christmas and we have guests. Let's just put it down to a slip-up and carry on. Alice seems level headed enough and Lily will hopefully keep Oliver occupied. Maybe I should distract Toby with a film this evening and keep him out of the way of everyone."

"Hmm, does this mean you won't be attending midnight mass?"

David grins. "If you insist, I'll stay here and keep the fire burning."

Pushing him playfully, I roll my eyes. "It's gas, you idiot. Anyway, perhaps mass is a step too far for this family. I'll go with Alice and Lily and hopefully, Oliver will sober up in time to come with us. Well, I should really get back and finish the dinner preparations. I'm pretty sure it's a charcoaled casserole by now."

As I turn to leave, David grabs my arm and says in a low voice. "You know, we could, um… make use of the privacy."

"What here – now?"

He pulls me close and whispers, "Why not?"

Pushing him away, I wrinkle my nose. "Because you're covered in sweat and knowing our luck, the whole family will come and find us in a compromising position. How on earth could we take the moral high ground then?"

Laughing, David follows me inside and I breathe a sigh of relief. Thank goodness we weathered that storm. Hopefully, that was just a blip on an otherwise glorious Christmas horizon. I hope so because more than anything, I want a nice family Christmas with no drama.

Alice is washing up when I venture back into the kitchen and I say gratefully, "I'm sorry, Alice, you shouldn't have to do that."

"Nonsense, why wouldn't I lend a hand, it's obvious you could do with one?"

I notice the room is empty which I'm grateful for and say in a low voice. "I'm sorry about all this. You see, we have a few family issues that need resolving and I hope they don't ruin things."

"You know, Florence. I am a good listener." Alice says kindly and I'm almost tempted to offload everything onto her extremely capable shoulders but something holds me back and I just smile brightly.

"I may hold you to that. Now, let's get this Christmas back on track and try to enjoy ourselves."

As we work putting the final preparations to the meal I planned weeks in advance, I feel a little empty inside. Alice works away but I still feel on edge around her. There is something about her that makes me feel as if she is judging me and not in a good way.

By the time dinner is ready, all I want to do is to curl up in a ball and cry myself to sleep but instead, I call up the stairs, "Dinner's ready."

Alice and I plate up the rich beef casserole and dumplings and we set a plate of vegetables on the table for everyone to help themselves. I look around with satisfaction because the table looks amazing. A starched white cloth, looks pristine underneath the crystal glasses and gold placemats. Candles burn surrounded by foliage creating an image of festive perfection. Soft Christmas music spills out from the hidden speakers and the fairy lights twinkle around the room making everything appear magical. A jug of elderflower crowded with ice cubes, causing a pleasant clinking sound when it pours, sits on the table and white napkins sit inside silver reindeer napkin holders that sparkle as they catch the light.

By the time we're ready there's still no sign of anyone and Alice says quickly, "Shall I hurry them up?"

"No, don't worry, I'll rustle the herd. Grab yourself a drink and help yourself, I won't be long."

Leaving Alice to it, I head upstairs to the cinema room and find David and Toby laughing at a comedy on the large television. They look up and smile as I shout above the noise, "Dinner's ready."

I leave them to make their way and head along the hallway to Oliver's room. I knock loudly and enter and smile when I see the two of them curled up in each other's arms as they sleep soundly on top of Oliver's bed. It's almost a shame to disturb them as I whisper, "Guys, dinner's ready."

Lily sits bolt upright and looks worried. "Oh, my goodness, how long have been asleep for?"

I smile as Oliver groans and blinks as the light in the hallway catches his eye. "Less than an hour. Come on, you don't want it to get cold."

Lily springs up to follow me and Oliver says, "I'll give it a miss, I feel terrible and couldn't eat anything if I tried."

Lily looks worried. "Maybe I should stay here with you, in case you're sick."

I feel irritated because Oliver has obviously brought this on himself and say sharply, "No, he can stay here and rest. You shouldn't have to miss out because of his mistakes."

Lily opens her mouth and I'm sure it's to defend him but Oliver says quickly, "It's ok, you go and enjoy your meal. I'll just watch some tv and hopefully be down later."

We leave him to it and as we head downstairs, Lily says in a small voice, "I don't think Oliver intentionally drunk the alcohol."

"What do you mean?"

She looks uncomfortable and says in a worried voice, "It may be nothing but Toby said he found a hip flask underneath Oliver's bed and it was almost empty. The thing is, Florence, I've been with Oliver all day and never saw him drink from it once. How could he have got so drunk without me knowing?"

I try not to think about what she's implying because I absolutely cannot deal with any more drama tonight, so I say quickly. "Well, it is what it is and we can't change it. Let's just hope it was a one-off and won't be repeated. Goodness knows what you and your mother think of us. It's not always like this, you know."

Lily smiles and my words sound false even to my ears as I say brightly, "Anyway, it's Christmas Eve. Let's just go and enjoy it."

Lily smiles and follows me into the kitchen and I watch as she takes the seat beside Alice. I notice she keeps her eyes lowered and feel bad. She obviously feels extremely uncomfortable now and I could kill Oliver. Despite what Lily says she just doesn't know him as we do. That little stunt had Oliver written all over it and I just pray he doesn't lose control again because I'm not sure if my nerves can cope with another confrontation.

24

Only Alice, Lily and I make Christmas Eve Mass. David and the boys had an early night, and I thought it was for the best.

As we walk up the small hill towards the church, Alice says with delight, "Look at the lovely candles lighting our way."

I smile as I see the little candles in glass jars lining the route. The night is crisp and clear and the stars shine out brilliantly against the inky blue sky. Lily laughs and points to the brightest one. "Do you think that's the star of Bethlehem?"

Alice nods. "I think it must be the one the shepherds saw that night. How amazing is it to think that we are seeing the same one now, decades later?"

Lily giggles and I smile. Alice turns to me and says gratefully, "Thank you for bringing us here. It always means so much to remember the true meaning of Christmas."

"To be honest, Alice I should be thanking you. You're right, we get so bogged down with the mechanics of it all we forget about the simple pleasures it brings. For instance, listen to the sound of the organ playing inside the church calling us in. There's something special about joining crowds of people to celebrate the reason why we are here at all and spending time with family and friends outside of the home is something special in itself. You know, I think this moment is what I will remember most about this Christmas. The simplicity of it all and the sense of anticipation that goes with it."

"And the cold." Lily shivers and pulls her coat a little tighter around her as she stamps her feet on the frozen ground.

"Yes, and the cold." I laugh and up my pace, so we at least get a seat in the unusually crowded church.

Inside is just as magical and I love seeing the church candles burning brightly on their stone ledges. There's an aura of reverence mingling with the excited chatter of a congregation looking forward to a service that will bring as much pleasure as it will understanding. The organ plays its haunting melody as we walk past the wooden pews that offer little physical comfort that is outweighed by the inner calm they will provide when the service begins. A slight musky smell invades my senses as centuries of traditions mix with modern-day foliage gathered from the fields outside.

We shift along to the end of a fast filling pew and huddle together, more for warmth than the space we need, to allow more people to fit inside.

As the service begins and the true magic of Christmas reveals itself, I pray hard for a happy Christmas with no more dramas.

CHRISTMAS DAY

6 am and I'm wide awake. Carefully, I reach for my robe and slippers before heading downstairs. I relish the silence of the early morning when the night turns to day, and the dawn is about to break on the most exciting day of the year. This is the moment I enjoy the most when everyone else sleeps and I get a few precious minutes of peace and tranquillity. I can enjoy the first cup of coffee of the day as I relish the moment when everything is in its place and it truly is the calm before the storm.

"Morning Florence."

I look across the room in surprise as I step into the kitchen and see Alice already sitting on the barstool at the breakfast bar with a steaming mug of coffee. "Happy Christmas." She smiles and says sweetly, "Would you like me to make you a coffee, the kettle's still hot?"

Feeling a little annoyed that I've been deprived of my 'alone time' I shake it off and return her greeting. "Happy Christmas to you too. Don't get up, I'll help myself."

"I'm sorry I couldn't sleep. I suppose I'm so used to getting up early it's a hard habit to break."

Nodding, I take the seat beside her. "Yes, a lie-in is a luxury denied to anyone cooking Christmas dinner."

We share the smile of two people who know exactly what trials and tribulations Christmas Day throws at them and Alice grins. "It's good to see you haven't been boiling the sprouts all night."

"Yes, I remember the soggy offerings at my own mother's table. It's no wonder I hated vegetables."

Alice looks around the clean and tidy kitchen. "Well, it certainly all looks ready. You have done an amazing job, Florence, I'm in awe."

"Don't be, I'm pretty sure any woman could achieve this level of perfection if it was all she had to concentrate her mind on."

Alice looks thoughtful. "I sense a change in the air for you next year."

"You and me both." I grin and see the understanding in her eyes. "You see, Alice, now the boys are all grown up, physically anyway, mentally the jury's still out on that one."

She rolls her eyes and I laugh. "However, I've been thinking that maybe it's now time for Florence Buckland. I need to find out who she will be in the future."

"What are you thinking of doing?"

"I'm not sure." I shrug and toy with my coffee cup. "I think I'll look for an assistant's role, something in banking perhaps where I was before I became a mother."

Alice stares at me hard and I feel a little uncomfortable. Then she says in a wistful voice, "I miss the little things that makes being a mother so fulfilling, don't you?"

I nod. "Yes. It's hard to go from being the centre of your children's universe to someone who just does their washing and subs their lifestyle. I long for the days when they really needed me."

"I agree. It's hard watching them grow up and inevitably away from you. I loved nothing more than feeling Lily's little arms cling to me and hear her high-pitched voice chattering excitedly. I miss the times she would snuggle up next to me as I read her a bedtime story and I miss doing all those things that children enjoy so much, like painting and pretend tea parties. I miss the surprise and excitement in her eyes on birthdays and Christmas and telling her off for doing things she should know better not to. I miss forming the little person I created because I can see now that she is the person I wanted her to be from the beginning."

I feel the tears behind my eyes as I share the same sentiments. "She's a credit to you, Alice. Such a sweet, caring girl who deserves only good things in life."

"Yes, she does and you know what it's like, Florence, as mothers, we only want the best for our children, even if they can't see it themselves."

Something about her tone of voice causes me to pay attention. There's a hard edge that creeps into it and I feel a prickle of something that takes me by surprise - fear.

Brushing it off, I laugh softly and stand. "Anyway, I need to get those sprouts on if we stand any chance of eating before nightfall."

Alice laughs and gathers our cups and takes them to the sink. "At least you have some help this year.

Just point me in the right direction and I'll do whatever you say."

"Thanks, you'll regret saying that."

As I head off to get ready, I wonder about the woman I left behind in the kitchen. I don't know what it is but there's something underneath the surface that sets me on edge. I can tell she disapproves of Oliver and his behaviour hasn't helped the situation but there's something else. I've caught her staring at us all individually as if she's working something out in her head. There's a familiarity to her that I can't quite place and it's as if there's an unspoken story waiting to be told. Maybe I'm just being over-sensitive because I'm so on edge, anyway. Having Toby and Oliver under the same roof is enough to send me to an early grave and maybe that's why I feel out of sorts.

As I shower and change, I shake off any doubts I have. It's Christmas Day after all and there is no time to dwell on fanciful nonsense.

25

"Morning, Lily."

"Morning, Florence, happy Christmas." I hand her a glass of orange juice and smile happily. "Did you sleep well?"

She nods and then looks up as Toby enters the room. I don't miss the flash of alarm that replaces the previous smile and feel a tension between them that wasn't there before. However, he just smiles and nods before enveloping me in a hug and whispering, "Happy Christmas mum."

Savouring the rare moment when my child actually hugs me without being asked, I say happily, "Thanks, son."

David looks up and grins. "What about your old man, are you too old to hug him?"

Laughing, Toby heads across and slaps him on the back and I watch with the ever-present mist behind my eyes as they hug it out.

I see Alice looking at them with approval and relax a little. Maybe this will all be fine after all.

Oliver soon surfaces and looks a little contrite as he smiles at everyone. "Morning, I'm sorry about yesterday, I'm not sure what happened but I feel great now."

He comes across and hugs me and then turns to Lily. "Morning gorgeous."

I watch as he lifts her hand and kisses it gallantly and I see the love shining in his eyes as she giggles and blushes prettily. I'm not sure why but I look at Toby and see the anger in his eyes and I sigh inside. Great, so much for my perfect day. Then I see Alice looking at Toby with interest and can tell she hasn't missed the look herself.

David wraps his arm around my waist and pulls me against him, whispering, "I can't wait to unwrap you later."

Giggling, I pull his lips to mine and whisper, "I'll hold you to that."

Pulling away, I turn my attention to making breakfast and switch the radio on so we can enjoy the sound of Christmas music.

Alice joins me and we set about making a lovely breakfast of scrambled eggs and smoked salmon with granary toast. This is our tradition and we substitute champagne with sparkling cider and it couldn't be any more perfect.

We always have a tradition of opening one present around the breakfast table on Christmas morning and I have already chosen the smallest gifts under the tree to put on each place setting.

By the time we all sit down, I am feeling happy and content and looking forward to a lovely day.

We tuck in and even Oliver and Toby put aside their differences for once. So far so good and as our attention turns to the gifts, I feel excited to see what everyone has.

"Open yours first, Florence."

David smiles as I take the small box and note the beautiful wrapping. "Well, you certainly didn't wrap this David."

Laughing, he holds up his hands. "Busted. Actually, I went to a little stall in the mall who were offering a gift-wrapping service."

I look at the present, appreciating the time and effort gone into making it look so amazing and then tear off the paper revealing a small velvet box. As I open the lid, I feel excited to see a small bracelet nestling among the cushion. My eyes shine as brightly as the silver as I place it on my wrist and say gratefully, "It's beautiful, thank you, David."

Quickly, I turn to Alice and say, "You next, Alice."

I can tell she feels a little uncomfortable which I can understand and smile encouragingly as she opens the small box wrapped in white. She pulls out a bottle of perfume and says with delight, "Thank you, it's lovely."

Breaking into the packaging, she dabs a little on her wrist and offers it to Lily who nods with approval. "It suits you, mum."

Alice hands her the small package by her plate and Lily giggles with excitement as she rips off the wrapping. Like me, she has a small velvet box and looks at it with barely concealed delight. Inside is a pretty compact mirror and Alice says quickly, "I had it engraved."

Turning it over, her eyes shine with gratitude as she reads, 'My best friend is my daughter.'

The writing is small and I can tell it means a lot as she turns and hugs her mother. "I love it, thank you."

Toby opens his and whistles as he pulls out a set of earbuds he has wanted for some time and Oliver laughs as he opens the exact same gift. "I might have known."

Alice looks confused and David laughs. "Florence always treats them exactly the same so there are no arguments. Even now they're almost men."

As David unwraps his, I smile to myself as he looks with excitement at the brand new watch I bought him. "Thanks, darling, it's just what I wanted."

As we clear away the breakfast things, I congratulate myself on a happy breakfast. Maybe this day will go well after all.

26

Oliver and I leave the rest to it and disappear to the cinema room after breakfast. I feel glad to escape what is turning out to be an extremely awkward situation. I could feel Toby's eyes burning into me from across the table as he watched my every move and I've no doubt that Oliver noticed.

As soon as we reach the cinema room, he grabs my arm roughly. "What's the story with Toby?"

Shaking him off, I say angrily, "Nothing."

He stares at me hard and I feel my face burning as he hisses, "Liar."

I feel a little scared because this Oliver is completely different to the one I love and once again, the doubts make another appearance as he paces the room. "I'm sorry, Lily but I don't believe you. For some reason he has this gloating look that he always has when he's got one over on me. You won't look at him and there's an atmosphere that I can't explain. What happened when I was ill yesterday and don't lie to me because I only have to ask him and he would be happy to tell me?"

I feel my legs shaking as I sit on the settee and put my head in my hands, saying in a whisper, "We kissed."

167

The silence scares me more than looking up because I feel such a failure. I have let Oliver down and couldn't feel any worse than I do now.

The settee sags as he sits beside me and I'm surprised when an arm wraps around my shoulder and pulls me close. He sighs, "I don't blame you. It wouldn't be the first time he's done this. But you should know that Toby is a compulsive liar. He will say anything to get what he wants and is good at it. I'm not surprised he targeted you, he could see how much I love you and what better way to get back at me than to damage my relationship with you?"

I stare at him in surprise. "You're not angry."

"Not with you, although I am disappointed."

I feel my face burn as he shakes his head and makes a fist. "That brother of mine, if you can call him that, has got it coming. I've put up with this for far too long. If he takes one more step out of line, I'm doing what I should have done all those years ago."

I almost don't want to know but say fearfully, "What?"

Oliver's eyes reveal the approaching storm as he hisses, "He won't look so pretty by the time I've finished with him."

Feeling as if I have to put a stop to this before it gets out of hand, I pull his lips to mine and kiss him with a desperation I have never felt before. As he responds in the same desperate way, I try to put my emotions in the right place. I love Oliver, not Toby.

168

I know I do. I need to make this right and distract him from ruining the day for everyone.

As Oliver's hands start to wander, I don't stop him. He needs me to show him how much I love him and even the thought of my mother nearby doesn't deter me. However, when Oliver kisses me it's Toby's face I see. When Oliver's hand touches me, it's Toby's touch I crave. I feel so conflicted because I have only shared a moment of time with Toby and months with Oliver. How is this possible and what on earth am I going to do about it?

It must be about twenty minutes later that a knock on the door has us guiltily rearranging our clothing and as the door opens, I feel relieved to see Florence smiling in the doorway. "Come on guys, we are going to open the presents under the tree."

Feeling a little guilty about what we just did, I almost run towards her and she laughs. "Someone's excited."

Oliver laughs and follows us downstairs and as we enter the living room, the first face I see is Toby's looking at me with a pained expression. I can't deal with my feelings for him, especially after what we just did, so I race over to sit beside my mother and don't miss the hard look she shoots Oliver as he follows me into the room and pointedly sits as far away from Toby as possible.

Florence hands around more brightly coloured drinks and says brightly, "Ok let's get started."

She hands out the gifts and soon the room is filled with laughter and cries of delight. I love my cashmere jumper and matching scarf and hat from Florence and David. Mum has outdone herself as usual and bought me way too many presents and by the time I reach a small gift from Oliver, I am feeling extremely spoiled.

As I unwrap the parcel, I look across at Oliver and smile as I unwrap his gift. Much the same as Florence's from breakfast, it's a small velvet box and my fingers shake as I open it. Inside is a shiny silver ring and I look up in surprise. "It's beautiful, Oliver."

However, the look he gives me is one of confusion as he makes his way across the room. Just before he reaches me, I notice the engraving inside the ring and see in tiny letters, *'Sadie and Oliver forever.'*

I drop the ring as if it burns and Florence says, "Is everything ok, Lily?"

I start to tremble as mum picks up the ring and reads the words, before saying tightly, "What's this?"

Oliver grabs the ring and studies it before staring at me in horror. "I've never seen this before in my life, Lily. I swear it's not mine."

I shake my head in disbelief as Florence says in a worried voice, "What's wrong – Oliver - Lily?"

I'm not sure what to say and just look at him with so much hurt I feel my heart-breaking. Oliver drops to his knees before me and takes my hands, saying with desperation, "I promise you, Lily, I never gave you that gift."

Mum picks up the wrapping and says coldly, "Then why does the label say, *to Lily with love from Oliver*? Is this not your handwriting?"

Grabbing the label, he stares at in disbelief. "Of course, it is, but this wasn't the present I wrapped."

Florence says loudly, "Will somebody please tell me what's going on?"

Toby interrupts, "What always happens. Oliver has obviously been caught out and is now trying to act as if he knows nothing about it."

Rounding on him angrily, Oliver shouts, "Shut the fuck up, who asked you anyway?"

"Oliver!"

David roars as Oliver says desperately, "Please, Lily, you've got to believe me, it isn't from me."

Something snaps inside me and jumping up, I shout, "Do you think I'm stupid, Oliver? Of course, it wasn't intended for me, it's got another girl's name on it. Tell me, have you been seeing Sadie behind my back and think very carefully before you answer me?"

You could hear a pin drop in the room as Oliver says loudly, "No! I'm begging you to believe me, Lily. I would never do that to you."

He looks so upset it's almost believable but then I remember Sadie racing down the staircase at the party looking so upset with Oliver following her. I hear all the whispers around campus as people tell me about his infidelity and I see the pain in my

171

mother's face as she implores me to wake up and see what's been staring at me for weeks now. In my heart I know Oliver is lying, he must be. However, as I see all the shocked faces around me, I know now is not the time to make a scene. There will be plenty of time for that later, so I just sigh and say in a small voice, "I believe you, Oliver."

Mum gasps and I feel bad as Oliver pulls me against him and says with relief, "Thank God. Please, believe me, Lily, I have never seen that ring before in my life."

Shrugging, I sit back down and reach for my drink as Florence says loudly, "Um… well… let's just carry on now that's cleared up."

I'm not sure that anyone in the room believes Oliver, me included, but it's difficult when you're in someone else's home and it's Christmas Day. Oliver and I can talk about this after Christmas because suddenly, the new year is not looking as promising for us as it did before we came here.

27

We left the rest of the gifts under the tree as Florence decided that dinner was now the priority. I feel bad for her as she tries to paper over the obvious cracks in her perfect day and calls us to sit down.

Mum helps her carry in the food and I try to get a grip. Oliver is looking so worried I could almost believe him and I catch Toby shaking his head and looking daggers at his brother, who is pointedly ignoring him.

David tries to rescue the situation and says loudly, "Ok, I'll carve the turkey, hand me your plates everyone, one at a time."

Luckily, the need for food takes away the awkward atmosphere and we are soon heaping our plates with turkey and all the trimmings. There is so much food, I wonder if we will eat it all and soon the sound of crackers fill the air as we attempt to get this Christmas back on track.

If somebody walked past and looked through the window, they would see a scene that's on repeat in every home around the country. Laughter, loud conversation and the sight of several people eating, drinking and enjoying each other's company. They would think these people have everything. It certainly looks that way but like the most carefully crafted scene, outward appearances can be deceptive. Scratch the surface of this perfect picture and you will see the ugly truth. Perfection comes at a cost and it's a price that can ruin lives. This is no exception because the people who eat at this table are more tainted than most.

Mum leans across and whispers, "Is everything ok, darling?"

I nod but I know she doesn't believe me. "If you want to leave, I can make our excuses."

I can tell Oliver is trying to hear what she says and his hand reaches for mine and squeezes it under the table. I feel sick inside and so conflicted I don't know which way to turn. On the one hand, I want to take my mother's hand and run back to where life is normal and without drama. On the other hand, I love Oliver and believe him when he says he never sent that gift. Then again, how could I be so stupid because if he didn't send it, then who did? Then if I do leave, it would also mean leaving Toby who looks as if he's in his own private Hell. My heart reaches out to him because there's something about him that speaks to my soul. He only has to breathe in my direction and I'm drawn towards him as if by magnetic force. What is it about Toby that intrigues me? Is it lust, attraction, or something much deeper? I find myself wanting to find out and suddenly it all gets too much and I scrape back my chair and say quickly, "I'm sorry, I need to use the ladies?"

As I race from the room, it's just to put some distance between me and the situation I'm in. I need to think and it's impossible to do it here.

By the time I reach the toilet, my mind is buzzing with everything that's happened. What do I do? Why has meeting Toby complicated my life so quickly and why do I believe Oliver in the face of so much evidence against him?

Five minutes later, a knock on the door interrupts my thoughts and I say quickly, "I won't be long."

My mother's voice says urgently, "Let me in, darling."

Sighing, I unlock the door and she steps inside looking concerned.

"Tell me what's wrong and I'll make it better."

"Tell you what?"

She appears annoyed and says curtly, "Oliver. He's not right for you."

Her words irritate me and I snap. "In your opinion."

"Which is usually right."

Shrugging, I place my hand on the door handle and laugh bitterly. "Listen, mum, this looks weird us being locked in the toilet together. Let's just go back to the table and try not to ruin the day for everyone else."

Her hand grabs mine and she pulls me back. "I couldn't care less about how it looks. I'm not leaving until I've said my piece."

Resigned to the lecture, I sigh and sit on the toilet seat. "Go on then."

Mum's voice is soft but harsh. "Wake up, Lily. That boy is bad news. Nothing he has done has been

175

normal and I think you know that. He lied about the alcohol and he wrapped the wrong gift and gave it to you. When I saw Nancy at the Mall, she told me some terrible things about the boy and I believe every word."

"What things?" My heart races as she spits, "Cheating mainly. Apparently, Sadie isn't the only one either. Nancy told me that the whispers around campus are true and nobody wants to be the one to tell you. Oliver is known to boast about it in the locker room and has told everyone who will listen what a pushover you are."

My blood freezes in my veins as she carries on relentlessly. "What she told me wasn't any surprise. When I met him, I saw it for myself. The cocky arrogance of a boy who likes everything his own way. I was prepared to give him the benefit of the doubt but when we came here, I saw him for the person he really is. He is disrespectful and cruel and the faces of his family when he is around reinforces my opinion. For some reason they are scared of him and what he may do and that was confirmed when I had a little chat with Toby yesterday."

I stare at her in alarm and whisper "What did he say?"

"That Oliver has always been a problem. Thinks with his fists and cares nothing for people's feelings. He's always made it his mission to ruin every relationship Toby has ever had and thinks nothing of stealing his girls, money and possessions on a regular basis. He is also prone to violence and word is…"

She breaks off and I say with a slight tremble to my voice, "What?"

I can't ignore the worry in her eyes as she whispers, "That he raped a girl."

The blood rushes to my head and I shake it vehemently, "Stop, you can't believe Toby, he hates Oliver and is just trying to split us up."

"Why would he do that, Lily?"

Mum's tone is ominous and I retreat into myself. "He just would, that's all."

Kneeling down before me, she takes my hand and says with a slight break to her voice, "Please, let's just get our things and go. I think you know things aren't right here. Oliver has many problems and you just aren't strong enough to deal with them. You need to distance yourself from this family because they have secrets we are better off not knowing about."

A sharp knock on the door causes us to jump and Florence says, "Is everything alright in there?"

Mum yells, "Sorry, Lily is feeling a little unwell. We're sorry to cause any trouble."

I feel bad as I hear the concern in her voice. "Oh no, I'm sorry, Lily darling. Can I get you anything?"

Mum looks at me hopefully and smiles reassuringly as I whisper, "It's ok, I feel much better now."

The look of rage that passes across mum's face sets me on edge and I jump up quickly and open the door, seeing Florence's anxious face outside. I laugh nervously. "I feel ok and just felt a little dizzy back there. Anyway, come on mum, we need to get back, we can't miss Christmas dinner."

I don't care that mum is shooting invisible arrows into my back. I don't care that she disapproves of Oliver and I don't believe a word she just told me. Oliver is not the bad person she spoke about, don't ask me how I know, I just do. And as for Toby, what is it about him that confuses me so much?

As we take our seats, I feel two sets of eyes burning into me and try not to catch either one. Toby or Oliver, which one is the right one? Oliver slips his hand in mine and whispers, "Are you ok, Lily flower?"

I almost want to cry because *no,* I am definitely not ok but just say in a bright voice, "Yes, of course, why wouldn't I be?"

Mum takes her seat beside me and I feel uncomfortable. I know she doesn't approve of my choices but I can't help that. I have lived so long in her shadow I need to break away to reach the light. She may have my best interests at heart but I have to face something I've been trying to ignore for several years now - my mum scares the hell out of me.

28

ALICE

Outwardly I seem ok. Inside, a rage is building that I am struggling to control. Why is Lily being so stubborn? What more can I do to make her see that Oliver is not the one for her? Nothing has worked. I thought the gift would have been the decider but the stupid girl believed his excuses and dismissed them out of hand. Why is she being such a doormat?

It was so easy. Meeting Nancy was a gift from the gods as she filled me in on what happened with Sadie Carmichael. I saw a way I could end this relationship with little effort on my part other than swapping a gift under the tree. When Lily visited her friend, I seized my chance and soon found Oliver's gift carefully wrapped. Luckily, it was of a similar size, so I carefully removed the Sellotape and substituted his gift with mine. I'm sure Lily would have loved the beautiful necklace he bought for her but that now lies in the bin outside, along with the other trash. Then there was the spiked drink. I thought that would be enough to show her what madness she was getting into. It was easy to add the tasteless vodka to Oliver's drinks while Florence's back was turned. Even that plan failed because my gullible daughter would excuse that man everything it appears.

As the conversation continues, I feel the walls closing in on me. I don't have long. Time is running out and I need to act fast.

I see Toby looking as if he wants to be anywhere but here and wonder about him. Outwardly he appears normal and a decent guy but I recognise the madness in his eyes. I'm not stupid because I have lived with the same madness for many years now. I watched as his eyes followed Lily as she climbed the stairs and noticed the hard edge creep into his expression before heading off to find his mother. I'm not stupid, something happened between them and Lily is such a gullible fool she probably believed everything he told her. It's obvious he's using her to get to his brother, which is why I need to end this once and for all. Lily will be part of this family over my dead body because there is more than the problem of Oliver haunting this family. They are broken and tainted and I don't want them anywhere near my little girl.

The food tastes like sawdust in my mouth as the day continues around me. As I help Florence clear the main course away, I wonder how on earth I'm going to get Lily to see sense without revealing the secret I've been guarding since before she was born.

"Alice, are you ok, you seem a little distracted?"

I turn to see Florence looking worried as she stands behind me and I smile. "Oh, don't worry about me, I'm just a little worried about Lily. She says she's ok but I know my daughter and she's trying to hide it."

Looking concerned, Florence whispers, "Leave it with me."

Turning around, she says loudly, "Listen, guys, maybe we should have dessert after the Queen's speech."

The men groan and she says firmly, "For goodness' sake, you can wait an hour or so. Let your dinner go down and take a break. The food will still be here later and you will probably enjoy it more, anyway."

She winks at me as she washes up and I say gratefully, "Thank you, I appreciate it."

"It's fine, to be honest, I am a little full and could do with letting the main course go down."

David wanders over and I watch as he bends down and kisses her lightly on the neck and she smiles making me envious of her. She has a husband who loves her and has probably never once thought about cheating on her. She has a loving family who idolises her, and she doesn't lie awake at night worrying about money and how she will afford to eat the next month. I curse my bad judgement in marrying a man like Peter who couldn't keep his trousers on. I blame him for the direction my life took when he cheated on me all those years ago and I blame his weakness for not providing for his family and gambling away any future we had. I don't want that for Lily. She cannot marry a man like that and Oliver *is* that man. I can tell because he's a player, just like Peter was.

181

Suddenly, I feel overwhelmed by the whole situation and say quickly, "If you'll excuse me, I may take a walk to get some fresh air."

Florence looks worried. "Would you like some company?"

"No, it's fine. Just once around the block will be all I need. We usually take a walk after lunch, anyway."

I don't miss the relief in Florence's eyes as I head outside. She is finding this as difficult as I am and it's probably because of her own set of problems she is struggling to disguise. It must be difficult pretending everything is ok when it's so obviously not.

Lily looks away as I walk past and I see the hurt in her eyes as she tries to disguise it. She won't have appreciated my words but I can't help that. I would rather she is angry with me until next Christmas than live a lifetime of regrets with Oliver who grates on my nerves everytime I see his smug face.

As I wrench open the front door, I take a deep breath and feel the pure air cleanse the toxic air of the house inside from my lungs. I need to think and clear my mind before it all unravels.

All around me the smart street is quiet. The snow is still falling and yet I don't feel the cold. My footsteps leave gaping holes in perfection as I tread along the path and the slight breeze that chills, sterilises my heart and causes my nerves to settle.

As I try to clear my mind the nightmare returns and I think back to when it all started to go so badly wrong.

As I enter the ward, the staff nurse calls me aside. "Can I have a word, Alice?"

Feeling a little apprehensive, I try to remember if I've given her cause to pull me up on anything, however the look on her face tells me it's serious so I steel myself for what she's about to say.

"Listen, we've got a situation that's pretty distasteful. There's a girl on the way in who's about to give birth and it may be pretty emotional."

"Why?"

She sighs heavily. "You know that serial rapist who's been plaguing the streets for months now?"

"I thought they caught him last week."

She nods. "They did but the girl on her way here in an ambulance is one of his victims and the baby..."

"Is his?"

"Yes, I'm afraid so. Her parents are strict Catholics and wouldn't allow her to have an abortion, so she's had to go through with it. Social services are standing by to take the baby into care and she has given express instructions she doesn't want to see, hear, or hold her baby."

Shaking my head sadly, I pity the poor girl. Not only has she been subjected to a terrifying ordeal but has had to live with the results for nine months while his seed formed another version of him inside her.

Maria sighs. "I'll deal with it but you know how mad it gets here. If I'm called away you need to be up to speed with everything. We must protect her at all costs and just hope the baby goes to a loving home."

She rushes off as is normal in this busy hospital leaving me feeling bad for the girl and the poor baby who will never know its mother.

Sighing heavily, I return to the couple who were admitted several hours ago. A nice, ordinary, decent couple who will make good parents. I just know they will because they appear sweet, kind and loving.

As I push the door open, I see the anxious face of her husband as he says fearfully, "She's in so much pain, nurse. Can you give her anything else?"

The woman looks to be in torment as the tears roll down her cheeks and I smile sympathetically. "Let me take a look and see what I can do."

As I check her out, I think about the two situations unfolding right now. One is how it was always meant to be, a loving couple bringing their first child into the world and promising it a happy future and the other an accident of nature that is unwanted, unwelcome and the spawn of the devil himself.

I read about the rapist, Victor Scott. He raped twelve girls in the space of six months and beat them up pretty badly too. The thought of him leaves

*a bad taste in my mouth as I imagine the terror
those poor girls went through. Even though he is
now languishing at her majesty's pleasure, it still
sickens me to think of him enjoying a warm bed at
night and a hot meal with none of the nightmares
those poor girls will be left with for the rest of their
lives. I just hope he receives some rough justice in
prison because it's nothing less than he deserves.*

*"Not long now Mr and Mrs Buckland, I imagine
your baby will be born within the hour."*

*Another contraction grips the woman hard and
her screams drown out her husband's request for
more pain relief.*

*Smiling sympathetically, I leave the room and
head off to check on the other couple next door.*

*It's a busy night and we are two staff down. We
have no time to waste and I feel bad for my patients.
They are not getting the care they need because of
the hospital cutbacks and I hate knowing that I'm
not delivering the care I would like to.*

*As the shift progresses, I look with interest at the
group of people waiting in the nearby waiting room
for the girl who arrived nearly an hour ago. My
colleague has dealt with her and I feel angry that
the impassive faces of the social workers stand by,
ready to sign the necessary paperwork to take the
newborn baby into the care of the state. Her father
and mother wait with them and speak in hushed
voices and I feel angry towards them. They can't
even be by her side when she needs them most
because of religion.*

The staff nurse rushes by and smiles wearily. "How are things with you, Alice?"

"Going like clockwork. My couple's child will be here soon and then I can lend a hand elsewhere."

"Great, I could certainly use some help, Typical this has happened when we are short-staffed."

As I return to the Bucklands, I feel angry that we have to work under this pressure. However, my anger will have to wait because the woman's scream greets me as I enter the room and her husband shouts, "For god's sake, she's in agony here. Do something!"

Ignoring him, I carry out my duties on autopilot as I've always done and set about delivering their baby.

It all starts out well enough. The observations are good and there are no complications that I can see. However, as the woman pushes and screams, I can tell by the monitor that something is wrong. I feel the panic set in as I see the heart rate decrease and yell at her to push harder. The crying in the room breaks my heart as she screams and pushes one final time and thankfully the baby follows before I need to call it in as an emergency. Quickly, I grab the baby and say to her husband, "I need you to cut the cord now if you want to because I have to whisk baby off to check he's ok."

"He?"

The tears pour down both of their faces as I tell them they have a son. Nodding, I repeat my request with some urgency, "Please, it needs to be now."

David Buckland rushes towards me and I will never forget the emotion in his eyes as he sees his son for the first time. He carries out the ritual as if in a trance and my heart lurches as his wife says anxiously, "Is everything ok, I can't hear him crying?"

David looks worried and I smile reassuringly, "He's fine, nothing to worry about. I'll clean him up and then you can meet your son properly."

Rushing from the room, I hold the little baby to my chest and pray he's ok. He is breathing but not crying and I need to act fast. As I head into the nearby room that we use to check the new babies, I fear for him. However, although he is weak, he is alive and I thank god for that. Maria races in with an identical bundle and looks exhausted. "All done. I just need to clean him up and pop him into special care until he can leave."

She smiles as she sees the little bundle in my arms and says, "All ok?"

Nodding, I say softly, "A little boy."

"It makes it all worthwhile, doesn't it?" She smiles and I laugh softly, "Yes, it certainly does." I look at the little baby in my arms and feel a surge of emotion for the small defenceless baby. Peering at him, she says quickly, "I don't like the look of his colour. Maybe we should get them both up to Neonatal and monitor them."

Nodding, I spring to attention, as the door opens and another staff member says, "Sorry, we have an emergency in room 50, breech I think."

The staff nurse says quickly, "Can you manage this, Alice? I'm sorry to ask but you can see how it is."

She rushes off leaving with me the two newborn babies and I think nothing about it until I reach the special care unit. Maybe it's intuition, or maybe it's because the Buckland's baby turns a colour I've seen before and I recognise the signs but as I hand them over, I do something I've never done before. I switch their identities.

As the special care nurse settles them into their incubators, I think about what I've done. What was I thinking? However, I just couldn't stand thinking of the lovely couple walking away without the baby they so obviously would love and cherish. I can't bear the thought of the gorgeous bundle of health and innocence being taken into care and never knowing what it was like to be normal because as the nurse confirms what I knew in my heart and presses for emergency help, I watch as the Buckland baby dies beside the innocent consequence of a maniac.

29

"Alice!"

Pulling myself back to the present, I shake off the past like an old worn coat as I have taught myself to do over the years.

Turning, I see Toby heading towards me and wonder what he wants. I'm not even sure how he found me and look at him quizzically as he approaches. Grinning, he nods towards the pavement. "I tracked your footsteps; I hope you don't mind."

"Of course not, um... but why?"

I feel curious because I can't think of a reason why he wants to talk to me, not one that I know about, anyway. He falls into step beside me. "You hate my brother, don't you?"

I feel slightly taken aback. "What makes you say that?"

"Because I recognise the signs. God knows I probably have that same look on my face when I see him most days, so it's easy to spot in others."

"So what if I do?"

He laughs softly. "I think I could help you, that's all."

"Help me with what?" I keep my cards close to my chest because I don't trust Toby. I'm not stupid and won't divulge any information to somebody who was a stranger to me a few hours ago.

He says bitterly, "He'll ruin your daughter's life, if he hasn't already."

His words feel like a knife to my heart, as I say sharply, "What do you mean, already?"

"Well, put it this way, she digs him and he pretends to dig her. She gets hooked on his line and he reels her in. Suddenly, she's spending more time with him than her studies and her grade average plummets. His never does because he's lucky in that department. Her friends are alienated because she just wants to spend time with him and that promising future she had is forgotten over the need to cling onto him."

I feel the anger bubbling like lava in a volcano and say sharply, "So what should I do?"

"Carry on doing what you're doing I suppose. I must say, I thought I was the only devious mind in that house until I saw your gift swapping trick. Genius, by the way. I thought my trick with the flask of vodka was good but spiking his drinks – brilliant."

"I don't know what you're talking about."

Toby laughs and holds up his hands. "Fine, keep your secret, it's not as if I care, anyway. However, I do care about your daughter."

"Why?"

He shrugs. "Ok, I don't but that's beside the point."

I think for a moment because Toby is surprising me. He is turning out to be quite a deviant and despite the seriousness of the situation; I like it.

He hunches his shoulders and says bitterly, "Oliver has always been the golden boy in our family. The best looking, the best at sports and the most desired. My parents dote on him because he is their blood whereas I am a constant reminder of their guilt."

"Their guilt?"

"Yes, guilt." His face twists and he spits, "That they caused my parents to die."

I feel shocked and he laughs a hollow laugh that makes me shiver. "Yes, the day he was born they were on their way to see him in hospital. A tanker hit their car, and they died instantly. I was sent to live with them because I wasn't much older than he was and David felt bad for losing his brother."

"They are your parents and you should show them some respect after the stable family home they have given you."

I didn't mean for my words to come out so sharply and Toby snarls. "Respect. Why should I? I didn't ask to live with them. I should have had my own parents to bring me up as it should have been. Because of their stupid baby, my parents left their own and came hurtling down the motorway. I'll never forgive any of them because I was left an orphan because of *them*."

Although I understand his anger and resentment, I also see what a loving home he was given and shake my head. "Let go of your hatred, Toby. By the sounds of it you've let it grow over the years and never dealt with it. David and Florence don't

191

deserve your anger and neither does Oliver. Nobody does because it was an accident. If you feel as if you're second best in that household, think again. I see the way Florence and David look at you. They love you just as much as Oliver, even more so."

He laughs bitterly. "Easy for you to say, you've known them for five minutes. No, I've had a lifetime to realise that it's all a front. Both of them are awkward around me and I know it's because I'm not really their son like *he* is. Well, I decided a long time ago that if my life has been ruined by them, then it was only polite to return the favour. I have enjoyed destroying Oliver at every opportunity and I know you want nothing more than to see the back of him yourself, so…"

I stare at him in surprise and feel the anticipation grow as he laughs softly, "If Lily won't listen to you, then tell her about the text messages he's been receiving."

"What text messages?"

Toby grins wickedly. "When Oliver was drunk, he left his phone downstairs. I tried but couldn't get into it but as it happens, I didn't need to. Several text messages from Sadie flashed on the screen in quick succession and I saw them on the display. I think they went along the lines of, 'We need to talk' and 'For god's sake, Oliver, just call me.' So, when you pulled that stunt with the ring, I figured you knew something about this Sadie and that got my interest. You see, Alice, it's become something of a game over the years."

"Game?"

"Yes, I try and destroy Oliver's life and he does mine."

"What's he ever done to you?"

"Hit on my girlfriends, told lies about me to my parents, blamed me for things that he did and played tricks on me just to get a response, so I can be punished for punching him when he started in the first place. You see, Alice, we have never got on because there is always this undercurrent of hatred running like Satan's river in our blood and this is my perfect chance to land the winning blow."

As he speaks, I pity him. Years of hatred has been left unchecked which has now grown like a cancer inside him. I recognise the madness in Toby because I have suffered the same fate. I almost pity him but then I have my own demons to deal with, so say coolly, "So, you want me to bring up the text messages making Lily confront Oliver?"

"Yes, he won't be able to hide this time and then she will see just what a despicable man she has given her heart to. It may not work; god only knows why she keeps on forgiving him but it's a shot at least."

"Ok, then, if you think it will work."
Toby grins. "Who knows but it will be fun watching him squirm. Anyway, I should get back before they miss me. Looking forward to the fireworks already."

He jogs away and I call, "Toby?"

He spins around and I say firmly, "You need to seek some help with your problem."

"I thought I just did."

He turns away and runs off leaving me with an uneasy feeling inside. Toby is heading for a lifetime of pain if he doesn't deal with this issue that's so deep-rooted inside him, it may overpower him in the end. I should know, I have the same one and as I think about the man who started this whole chain of events, I feel sick. Victor Scott has unknowingly destroyed many more lives than the poor girls he raped all those years ago. I thought I was doing the right thing when I swapped his baby for the Buckland's. I did it because I thought it was the right thing to do but now it's come back to bite me and drawn blood. How can I possibly allow my daughter to be in any kind of relationship with the child of a rapist? Oliver must have inherited some of his DNA and could become this violent, cold-blooded monster that his father was.

As I think about the sweet innocent face of my little girl being another one of Victor Scott's victims, I almost scream with fear. No, whatever happens I must protect Lily as I've always done. She comes first and my love for her knows no boundaries, which is why I will put a stop to this madness once and for all.

30

When I return home, Florence meets me at the door looking anxious. "Oh, there you are, Alice, is everything ok?"

"Of course, it couldn't be better."

She helps me off with my coat and smiles with relief. "Good. Now, come in and I'll make you a hot drink. It's freezing out there."

She shivers and I smile as I follow her into the warm, inviting kitchen. I see Lily and Oliver curled up watching television, and she doesn't even look up; just snuggles in closer to him. He is stroking her back while laughing at something on the tv and ordinarily I would love seeing her so happy. On the face of it, Oliver appears the perfect boyfriend. He is always attentive to her needs and loving in the way he treats her. However, I see the pain in her eyes when she thinks no one is looking. He has this dark side to him that bothers me and it's that feeling I hold on to as I sit down and plan my next move.

Toby is looking at his phone and doesn't make any eye contact and David is almost asleep as he sits slumps in his favourite armchair.

Florence hands me a warm mug of coffee and says loudly, "Ok, I think there are still some presents under the tree. Maybe we should open them and afterwards sit down for dessert."

She gets a few grunts from the men and I notice that Lily smiles sweetly at her and nods. As Florence hands the rest of the gifts out, I take the one she offers me and smile my thanks. "You are so kind, Florence. I really didn't expect so many gifts."

She shakes her head. "I love to give rather than receive. It's something that gives me a lot of pleasure, so you are very welcome."

I unwrap the beautiful silk scarf she has boxed up beautifully, and she says anxiously, "I have the receipt if it's not your colour."

"It's perfect, thank you."

Suddenly, we hear a gasp and David jumps up as if he's had an electric shock. Florence says, "What is it, David?"

He says angrily, "Is this a joke because it's not funny?"

We all look and see a rather large bottle of gin lying on the floor amid the brightly coloured wrapping, and he turns to Oliver with a hurt expression. "Answer me, Oliver, is this a joke?"

Oliver looks confused. "What are you talking about, it wasn't from me?"

"Then how do you explain the fact it says, 'to dad, with love, Oliver?' It's also your writing, your paper and your cruel gift. Why, are you doing this?"

Oliver jumps up and grabs the packaging and then looks at Toby and yells, "I told you it wasn't me. I'm guessing the real culprit is sitting there looking smug."

196

He makes towards Toby who is looking concerned and shaking his head as Florence steps between them and yells, "Enough! This ends now."

She turns to Oliver and the anger on her face sucks all the goodwill out of the room leaving nothing but disgust and recriminations. "How dare you, Oliver. Of course, this was you because why would anyone else be so cruel? For some reason, you have made it your mission to ruin this Christmas for everyone and I don't know why? How dare you use your father's illness against him just to play a trick, what's got into you?"

Oliver looks upset and I feel the victory heading my way when I see the pure disgust in Lily's eyes as she stares at him. "But I promise it wasn't me, I know it looks that way, but I didn't do it?"

He turns to David, "Please, it wasn't me, you've got to believe me."

Toby snorts. "Why would we believe anything you say? You've always been a compulsive liar, and this is no exception."

"Shut the fuck up, Toby. I know you did this. It's got your stamp all over it."

Toby laughs. "Actually no, it has *your* stamp all over it because, as mum pointed out, that's your handwriting."

"But not what I wrapped up. I bought dad a bottle of his favourite aftershave."

Toby laughs bitterly, "No Oliver, dad used to wear alcohol as his favourite scent but not anymore."

Lily gasps as Florence shouts, "Toby, how could you? Apologise to your father for that remark."

I see the fire burning in Toby's eyes as he turns to face his father and say tightly, "I'm sorry dad."

Maybe I'm the only one who detects the sarcastic edge to his tone because they leave it there and David turns to Oliver and says coldly, "I think you need to explain yourself."

"Why, I've done nothing wrong?"

"You never do." Toby says bluntly and Florence shouts, "Enough, this ends now, whatever it is. I've had it up to here with the lot of you. What must Lily and Alice think of us, all this bickering has got to stop?"

Lily looks uncomfortable as Oliver pulls her up and says tightly, "Come on, Lily, I need to get some fresh air."

Lily looks around and I can see she feels conflicted and as she catches my eye, I shake my head with disapproval and say, "Don't go with him, Lily."

The others look at me in surprise and I say firmly, "You need to think about what type of man you have given your heart to. Is this the sort of man you want to spend time with and invest in a future that could end up being one of smoke and mirrors because trust me, I've been there?"

Florence looks angry but before she can jump to her son's defence, I say bluntly, "Ask Oliver about the text messages he's been receiving from Sadie Carmichael." I hold my breath because this is a gamble that may fail terribly. I catch sight of Toby's face and he can barely conceal the delight in his eyes as he watches carefully for Oliver's reaction. "What messages? You're all mad and obviously just want to make me look bad. Come on, Lily I've had enough of this, someone is out to get me and no prizes for guessing who?"

He rounds on Toby angrily. "This is all you, Toby, it's got your devious mind written all over it. What's the matter, didn't your little trick work when you tried to steal Lily away from me?"

Florence looks confused as Lily turns bright red. "What do you mean – Toby?"

Toby shrugs. "It's not my fault if she's so desperate to get away from you, she'll take the first offer going."

Lily looks mortified and stares at him with such a hurt expression it makes the breath still in my body. "It was just a game?"

Her voice sounds shaky and reminds me of the little girl she once was and I want to murder Toby on the spot for bringing her so much pain.

He laughs. "Sorry, darling, you made it so easy for me. You see, Oliver has always made it his business to steal my girlfriends, and it was fun to do the same. No hard feelings, it was a nice kiss."

Florence gasps as David shouts, "Toby, how could you be so cruel?"

He shrugs, "Why not, it's not as if I actually care for any of you."

I almost can't look as Florence bursts out crying and sobs, "Why Toby, why do you hate us so much?"

Even I can feel the years of resentment seeping from the cracks in the walls and floor beneath our feet as Toby snarls, "Because you stole the most important thing a child ever has in their life – their parents."

David turns white as Florence cries, "We weren't responsible for their accident."

Toby snarls, "If you hadn't had *him*." He points angrily at Oliver, "Then they would never have been on the road that day. Yes, I blame you all because if he had never been born then they would still be alive today."

Florence makes towards him with the tears running down her face but he holds up his hand. "Keep away because I don't want you. I don't want any of you, I just want them. All my life I have known I was just a cuckoo in the nest. You gave me a home out of pity for me and to brush away your own guilt for causing it in the first place. I have always known that Oliver was your real son and not me which is why I resented him. He has that bond with you, he will always be a part of you and have that place in your heart only reserved for blood. I've grown up never feeling as if I belong and yet golden boy over there can do no wrong. I was never allowed to get to know my own father because *you* took that away from me. My own mother never got to see the child she created grow into a young man and you have robbed me of what was always meant to be my life. I will never forgive any of you, I hate you all."

There's a shocked silence as everyone looks at Toby and then David speaks up and says in a beaten voice, "Toby, I think there is something you should know."

Florence rushes to him and says urgently, "David, no!"

He takes her hand and says gently, "No, Florrie. We need to get this out in the open once and for all. He needs to know the truth."

I think the whole room holds its breath as David turns to Toby and says in a broken voice. "I am your real father, Toby."

31

You could hear a pin drop in the room as Florence cries softly and Toby's face is a picture of shock. "What do you mean?"

David sits down and shakes his head. "Sit down, all of you."

The only sound in the room is that of Florence crying as David says sadly, "I'm not proud of myself but you need to know the truth. Maybe we should have told you from the start. I suppose I wanted you to always think of your parents as the two, good, loving people they were."

I can see Toby shaking as David continues. "To put it bluntly, I had an affair with my brother's wife – your mother. It lasted for three years and I am not proud of what I did."

Toby stares at him in disbelief as Oliver heads across and puts his arm around his mother's shoulders.

David shrugs, "Florence and I were facing our own problems and Nicola was always willing to listen. Harvey and I had a difficult relationship, much like yours and Oliver's and never really saw eye to eye. As our problems grew, so did my dependence on Nicola until we both gave in to our feelings. Then she fell pregnant, and we both knew it was mine."

"How did you know, it could have been my father's?"

202

Toby's voice sounds strangled with emotion as David shakes his head. "It could have been and at the time we never knew for sure. When you were born Nicola went behind Harvey's back and sent off a sample of your DNA. She couldn't live with the guilt because by then our affair had ended because Florence had fallen pregnant with Oliver and it was the right thing to do."

I look across and see Oliver staring at the floor looking as white as a sheet. David says, "I'm so sorry, all of you. It was foolish and weak and I betrayed everyone just to get what I wanted."

I can see Florence's shoulders shaking as David says softly, "Florence – your mother, found out and confronted me. She was pregnant and vulnerable and for a while, I thought she would lose the baby."

Oliver sobs as Toby hisses, "You bastard."

David nods. "I was and nobody knows that more than me. So, you see, Toby, the day that Oliver was born, my brother found out the truth. He discovered the DNA results where Nicola had hidden them and confronted her. She confessed to everything which is why they were on the road that day. Not because I called them and asked them to come but because Harvey was in such a rage, he couldn't wait to have it out with me. He drove like a madman and I can only imagine how terrifying that journey must have been for Nicola because the tanker didn't hit your parents, Toby, Harvey hit the tanker."

The shock in the room is palpable as Toby's world crumbles to the ground for a second time. He shakes his head from side to side and says on repeat, "No... no... no... no!"

Then he says in a strangled voice, "You're lying."

Florence sits beside him and says softly, "It's true, darling. We didn't know they were coming and when David – your father, found out, it destroyed him."

"But how did you know what happened? You're making it up to make yourselves feel better."

Toby yells and Florence cries, "Because of the message we found on our answerphone when we returned home. Harvey yelled that he knew and was coming to confront David. He called him every name imaginable and we could hear the rage in his voice and your mother crying in the background. The police reports confirmed that he was driving erratically and swerved into the path of the tanker. The rest you know but you see, darling, you are David's son by blood, just as much as Oliver and he couldn't love you any more than he does. We both do."

"Why, how can you love me when I am a reminder of what he did?"

"Because sometimes love overpowers even the most terrible of sins. How could I not love you, Toby? When I saw your beautiful, sweet, innocent face, looking up at me from the crib, I fell in love immediately. I know that people do things they regret in life but sometimes you have to accept them and move on. I have always loved you with the fiercest kind of love there is because I wanted you to have the world. I am not your mother by blood but I am in every other way. I will never stop loving you and trying to make the world a better place for you. I will never turn my back on you because, until my dying day, I will put you before my own needs. You can hate me, but I will always love you because I *am* your mother in my heart. You *are* my child and that will never change. It is possible to have unconditional love for somebody who isn't a part of you because I have that for you, Toby and no matter what happens next, I want you to know I will always be your mother."

Toby looks wrecked and David says in a broken voice. "I couldn't deal with the guilt. I blamed myself for my brother's death and had to live with the knowledge he hated me in the moments before he died. If you want to blame anyone for their deaths, blame me because I have blamed myself ever since. Alcohol was the only cure for the pain and I needed a lot of it to deal with mine. You see, I am a weak man because where Florence shone in a moment of darkness, I failed. I failed her, my brother, Nicola and you. I failed Oliver for not being a strong role model and I failed myself. If you hate anyone, let it be me because you couldn't hate me any more than I hate myself."

Toby looks destroyed and I feel worried about what he will do. For someone who has lived with the resentment all these years, this could send him over the edge into madness.

It feels awkward, so I say gently, "Lily, we should leave them to talk this through. Come with me and pack your things."

I make to stand and Oliver says, "No, please stay, Lily, don't go."

Florence says through her tears, "No, please stay. I'm so sorry you had to hear that. Please stay though, it's Christmas day."

Lily looks conflicted as I say firmly, "No, you need to be alone. We're only in the way and should go."

Lily nods and makes to stand but Oliver yells, "No, I need you to stay. Lily, please don't go."

I feel so irritated, I snap, "Why do you need Lily so much, Oliver, when it's obvious you have another girl on speed dial."

The silence hits the room once again as Oliver looks confused. "What do you mean?"

"Ask him about the text messages he's been receiving from Sadie Carmichael, Lily. Let's see him explain them. He never gave you the chance earlier, so now is the perfect time."

Oliver looks confused and shakes his head. "What are you talking about? There's nothing going on with Sadie and me."

I see the doubt in Lily's eyes as she says in a small voice, "Then prove it."

He looks shocked. "Don't you believe me?"

Lily shrugs. "I don't know what to believe anymore. If you are telling the truth, you have nothing to worry about, so prove it, show me your messages."

I feel proud of my little girl as she stands her ground and looks Oliver defiantly in the eye and I see the attention in the room has switched to Oliver as he yells, "Fine but don't blame me for what you'll discover."

He reaches for his phone and scrolls to the messages and hands the phone to Lily. I catch the triumphant look in Toby's eye as she reads them and her face falls.

"Oh my God."

I watch in horror as the tears fall and feel the anger burning a hole in my reasoning as I shout, "You bastard, what have you done?"

Florence gasps, "Alice, for goodness' sake, don't speak to him like that."

"Like what? He deserves much worse."

Florence stands up her eyes blazing. "How dare you speak about Oliver like that? Look, I know you don't like him but quite frankly, I've had enough of your sly little digs and disapproving stares. Oliver has done nothing to hurt Lily, in fact, she's the one who hurt him because obviously she's a little tramp who would even cheat on him with his own brother when he's lying ill in bed."

I raise my hand and strike Florence across the face and she gasps with pain as I yell, "Don't you dare speak about my daughter like that. She is not to blame in any of this and we are leaving now - forever. Say goodbye, Lily."

David stands and yells, "How dare you hit my wife after all that she's done for you - get out."

"Don't worry, we're going. Come on, Lily."

I turn and see Lily standing watching us, with tears running down her face as she holds Oliver's phone in her hand and he looks as if he's about to cry. "No, I'm not going anywhere with you."

I stare at her in shock. "What do you mean, of course you're coming with me? Why would you stay here with these – *people*?"

"Because I love Oliver and if I'm certain of anything, it's that."

I watch in disbelief as she slips her hand in his and says softly, "I'm sorry, darling. I let you down and I will never forgive myself."

He looks at her with such happiness it sends me delirious as I shout, "No, you can't love him, he's a monster. What about the other girls, what about the drinking and disrespect he shows his family? What about the hurt in your eyes when he forces you to do things, what about the fact he's destroying your life because he demands your time when you should be studying? What about the friends you have lost because of *him*?"

I break off to get some much-needed oxygen, leaving the final nail in his coffin where it should remain – hidden. Lily says sadly, "I'm sorry, mum. I know you don't think Oliver is good enough but you're wrong. You don't see how amazing he is with me when we're alone. You don't see how kind and caring he is and how just the little things he does makes my heart burst. He isn't perfect but then none of us are, however, he's perfect to me because he has never let me down, contrary to what anyone else thinks."

"But Sadie Carmichael, what about her?"

Lily shrugs. "These text messages aren't what you think."

"Then what are they?" I hear the hysteria in my voice and realise I'm in danger of unravelling right before their eyes as Lily turns and says, "I think I'll let Oliver explain as it's so obvious you all think the worst of him."

Oliver looks surprised and then seems resigned to telling us whatever secret he's been hiding but as he opens his mouth to speak the doorbell rings.

Florence looks worried as she rushes to answer it and we all sit looking at one another in silence as we contemplate what just happened.

Florence returns with a woman who looks anxious and Florence says apologetically, "I'm sorry, Alice but could you go with Celia? Her husband Blake isn't feeling well, and she's worried he may be coming down with a stroke or a heart attack."

Feeling annoyed at her choice of words, I jump up. "Of course, but you don't come down with these, Florence. It's not like catching a cold or anything."

Florence colours up but I couldn't care less. I don't need her to be my friend. I just need her to stay as far away from me as possible and that includes Lily. As I head past her, I say quickly, "I won't be long, will you be ok?"

Her eyes flash and she says tightly, "Why wouldn't I be?"

Despite the seriousness of her situation, I see a spark of interest in the woman's eyes who I immediately dislike on sight. She is everything I hate in a person, cool, poised, immaculately groomed, with the look of a woman who thinks everyone is beneath them. To be honest, this is the last thing I want to do but I am a nurse and it's what I've been trained in.

As I follow her, I resolve that the next time I leave this house, it's with our bags packed and Lily firmly by my side.

32

LILY

I think I can breathe again. As mum follows Celia out, there's an audible sigh of relief in the room. She makes everything so tense and as if the situation wasn't bad enough; she makes it a hundred times worse.

Florence returns from showing them out and shakes her head. "Poor Blake, I hope he'll be ok."

David nods and Toby says irritably. "What about us, do you think we will ever be ok?"

I almost can't look at him because my anger towards him is so intense I want to hit out at him. He started this whole thing and I can't believe that he blamed his family for something that was so obviously out of their control.

Florence says awkwardly, "Hmm, well, anyway, I think we all need to calm down and maybe that was just the distraction we needed. Maybe I should fix us all a nice cup of tea while we wait for Alice."

Toby slumps back in his seat and looks so devastated it's difficult to watch. David looks broken and Oliver looks as if he's about to cry. Feeling bad for all of them, I say to Florence, "I'll make the drinks. You should maybe have some privacy after, um… what just happened."

211

To my surprise, she looks at me with tears in her eyes and says softly, "I'm sorry for calling you a tramp, Lily. I don't think you are and it was just the heat of the moment. Can you forgive me?"

"Of course. You were defending your son and nobody could blame you for that. I think a lot of things were said that come with a ready-made apology attached, let's just forget about it."

She smiles gratefully and I slip out of the room and take a deep breath. I feel so sorry for all of them. What a bombshell and it makes my problems with Oliver look nothing compared to theirs.

As I think about him, the tears build. How could I have doubted him? I should have known deep in my heart because actually he hasn't put a foot wrong. I listened to my own paranoia and other people's opinions before asking him outright and I'll never forgive myself because ultimately it led *me* to be the one to betray him.

I feel so incredibly stupid that I didn't just talk to him about my fears because the fact I kissed his brother will always be between us. Having seen the result of what that can do in the other room, it's definitely a wake-up call and I vow never to make the same mistake again. Thinking about Toby, I wonder why I was so drawn to him? The only reason I can think of is that he appeared a lot like me. We both had parents lying in the cold, hard ground and a part of us lies in there with them. We are both a little lost and maybe it was the uncertainty I felt over Oliver that drove me to do something so reckless.

Then there's my mother and as I think about her I can't breathe. She looked so angry and when she attacked Florence; I saw a side to her that scared me. Her eyes were those of a maniac and if there's one thing I know, I'm not leaving with her. No, Oliver is my future, and she had better deal with it because we are about to blow her world apart.

As I put the final touches to the drinks, Oliver heads inside the kitchen and looks so beaten I immediately run to him and wrap my arms around him. He visibly relaxes and slumps against me and holds me so tightly I almost can't breathe. I mumble, "I'm so sorry, darling."

"What have you got to be sorry about?"

"Toby - doubting you - what happened with your parents, it's quite a list to be going on with, don't you think?"

He squeezes me tightly. "I don't know what to think anymore. What just happened, well - it will take some getting used to. It's bad enough discovering your dad cheated on your mum but to have a baby with that woman and then my mother bringing it up as her own, well, I have a new-found respect for her."

"Yes, she's a strong woman, that's for sure."

Pulling back, he looks at me anxiously. "We're good though, aren't we, Lily?"

My eyes mist over. "Of course, but it should be me asking that question, not you."

He strokes the side of my face and I see the love shining from his eyes as he says gently, "I love you, Lily. I'm sorry that you discovered how much the way you did but it can't be helped."

Any further conversation stops because we jump apart as the door slams and we hear my mother say angrily, "Where are they?"

Sighing, I look at Oliver. "Well, round two I suppose."

He whispers, "Stay strong. I'm with you all the way."

Oliver grabs the tray and follows me into the living room and I see my mother looking irritated as she answers Florence, who is obviously concerned about Blake. "Stupid people. He had too much to drink and had indigestion on top of it. I had to firmly tell them not to call an ambulance because they may distract them from somebody who really needs it."

She looks at us entering the room and her eyes flash with anger. "I think you were about to explain something to us, Oliver. Well, I'm waiting."

Florence gasps at her rudeness and I see a side to my mother that fills me with shame. She appears not to care that she is rude, abrupt and so wrong about Oliver I will enjoy watching her eat humble pie.

As I hand out the drinks, I don't make eye contact with anyone and then sit beside Oliver as he begins to explain the text messages.

Everybody looks at him expectantly as he clears his throat and says softly, "The messages from Sadie aren't what you think they are. It was at a party one night that I came across her crying in one of the bedrooms. I passed the door, and it was open and saw her sobbing on the bed. I felt a little awkward but couldn't just walk past, so I went inside. She was a wreck and a little incoherent but after a while she calmed down when she realised I wasn't going anywhere and told me that Dean Fellowes had broken up with her. It surprised me because I didn't even know they were going out but then again, that's just the sort of guy he is. He uses and abuses women and then moves onto the next one. I thought nothing of it until he started showing the guys in the locker room a video he made of him and Sadie having sex. He thought it was hilarious and when I confronted him, he laughed in my face and told me I was just jealous and should get in there myself because she was so easy. I saw red and grabbed his phone and slung it against the wall, cracking the screen. The coach came in before we got into a fight but I knew it was just a matter of time. It didn't take long before Lewis did what he promised and sent the video to every member of the team, me included. Sadie found out and sought me out at that party we went to before Christmas. Lewis had already moved on to his next victim and Sadie was in bits over the video. I tried to calm her down and told her I would personally see to it that the video was destroyed and I'd support her by reporting him to the Dean. It's a criminal offence and he would be in a lot of trouble. Well, Sadie was so grateful for my help because I was the only one she told because she felt so embarrassed. She wanted to help me and as it turns out, she was the perfect person to help me with a Christmas gift for Lily."

My eyes mist over as I think of what they did and I hate myself all over again. He looks at me and hesitates and I nod. "Tell them."

Sitting beside me, he takes my hand in his and says softly, "I wanted to get Lily a ring. I know we haven't been together long but I know I love her. I know I want her in my life forever and when we leave Uni, I want us to set up home together."

Mum jumps up snarling, "Over my dead body, she is not leaving to live with you."

"Sit down and let him speak!"

David roars so loudly it makes us all jump and mum faces him with fire in her eyes. "How dare you speak to me like that you... adulterer?"

Florence rises to defend her husband and Oliver says loudly, "Shut up, all of you!"

He turns to face my mother and says dismissively, "In case you've forgotten, Lily is now an adult and can do whatever she wants. Anyway, where was I? Sadie's father owns a chain of jewellers and when I explained what I wanted; she was happy to help. She helped me design the ring and then took it to her father. The text messages regarded that ring because we were desperate to

216

have it made in time for Lily to open on Christmas day. When I didn't respond to her messages, she was anxious because she wanted to drop it in personally. However, as you all know, things haven't been great around here, so I missed her and she left for the Cotswolds with her family for Christmas. So, when Lily unwrapped that ring, I knew it wasn't the one I intended for her. What does need clearing up is, who did?"

I look at my mother because I already know and say softly, "It was you, wasn't it, mum."

Shrugging, she laughs bitterly. "I had to do something to make you see what he's like. Nancy told me about Sadie and if you believe that fanciful story, then you're a gullible fool."

I've had enough and shout, "If I'm a gullible fool, it's because of you!"

It's as if my words physically strike her because she sits back and looks at me with devastation. "Me?"

"Yes, you. All my life I've lived with a woman who scares me. Yes, scares me, mum. You may not realise it but you have no filter where it concerns me. I was afraid to tell you if I was in trouble with bullies or teachers because you would go down there all guns blazing and make the situation much worse. I had no friends because of you. I mean, who wants to play with a kid whose mother gets them in trouble for the smallest thing. Then there were any boyfriends I brought home. You made it perfectly clear you didn't approve of them and the things you

217

did, such as reporting one of them to the police for drinking, threatening another that you'll report him for rape if he dares even touch me, god, the list goes on."

I take a deep breath and say sadly, "Well, it's over, mum. I can't live like this. I want what Oliver's family has. They have a loving home and yes, they have problems but ultimately, I know they will work them out because that's what families do. They work through their problems and don't involve the authorities. Anyway, Oliver has shown me the direction he wants our relationship to go in and as it happens, I am more than happy about it."

Mum's face is ashen as she hisses, "And what direction is that exactly because from the looks of things, you're on a road to humiliation and pain with that one?"

Oliver interrupts. "The ring I had made is an engagement ring."

He drops to one knee in front of everyone and takes my hand. "Lily, will you marry me?"

As he says the words, my world rights itself. All the self-doubts, pain and accusations float away and are replaced with love and the realisation that I have found my destiny. There is silence in the room as I whisper, "Yes, Oliver, I will marry you."

Suddenly, mum makes a sound that causes my blood to freeze as she howls in pain like a wounded animal. "Noooo, Lily no, please God, no!"

We all stare at her in shock as she screams, "Not him, oh God, please not him. Lily, I'm begging you, don't do this, we can work it out but please no!"

She sobs, and it's as if her heart is broken. I feel alarmed as Florence rushes towards her, "Alice are you ok, it's not that bad, surely?"

"Bad, did you just say bad you stupid woman, it's worse than you'll ever know."

I stare at her in confusion and say with embarrassment, "For god's sake, mum, you're embarrassing me."

Suddenly, she laughs like a maniac and points at Oliver. "Look at him standing there so smug. Well, I've seen that face a million times in my nightmares and I will not stand by and watch my daughter make the mistake of her life."

David says loudly, "I think we all need to calm down and get everything into perspective."

Mum just laughs again and points at Oliver, snarling, "I will never be ok with him in your life, Lily because of who his father is."

Florence gasps and rushes to her husband's defence. "How dare you, David is a good, kind, caring husband and father? Lily would do no better than to meet a man such as him."

Laughing like a madwoman, mum screams, "Not him you stupid bitch, his real father."

33

The confused faces around me make me think my mother has gone mad as she cries. "I knew this would come back to haunt me. All these years I've lived wondering if I did the right thing and now I know I didn't."

She turns to Florence and David and shakes her head. "Your baby died at birth; you don't remember me but I was the nurse who delivered your son."

The whole room gasps and I watch as Florence steps back as if she was physically punched. David looks destroyed and says roughly, "You're lying."

Oliver stands as still as a statue beside me and I reach for his hand that feels like cold, hard ice, in mine. Mum carries on relentlessly. "Yes, your son is the result of a wicked sin that happened all those years ago. He is only here because a vile man raped a poor young girl and she was unable to terminate her pregnancy because of religion. She didn't want him and when your baby died, I switched them."

"What did you say?" Florence whispers so softly it almost can't be heard and mum yells, "Don't you see, I did what I thought was right. You…" She points at Oliver who is now shaking. "You are the result of a violent rape on a poor young woman who couldn't defend herself. She wasn't the only one either, and that man was caught and lived in prison until they found him with his throat cut one

220

morning. A fitting end for a monster and I should never have interfered. I should have let them take you into care but no - I wanted to help you and swapped you with their dead baby."

Florence sobs. "Please, stop saying that. Please!"

She starts to weep and David puts his arm around her visibly shaking himself, as Toby shouts, "So you're the cuckoo in the nest, not me. How does that feel, little brother?"

"Toby, for fuck's sake show some compassion for your brother." David's voice is stern but I can tell he is struggling to understand what's just happened.

"Brother, that's a laugh; no, as it turns out, he is just the product of filth which explains everything."

I've heard enough and shout, "Stop! For God's sake, mum, haven't you done enough damage? Please, just go."

"Go, I would like nothing more but you're coming with me, young lady. Don't you see that I can't leave you with such a man? It's in his DNA, he is violent, we already know that and I'm guessing if he doesn't get what he wants, he'll take it anyway. No, I can't take that chance with you."

"Stop it, oh God, please just stop. I'm going nowhere with you. I'm staying with Oliver and that's an end to it. If you make me choose, I'll choose him."

"Why him, Lily? Why him over your own mother's advice? You have known him five minutes compared to a lifetime with me and I have always

221

done my best for you. He won't. As soon as he's bored he'll be off and destroy your life before he goes. Listen to me, Lily, I'm your mother and I know best."

I can't bear it anymore, this has to stop, she is scaring me so much and so, I raise my hand and say gently, "Please sit-down, mum."

The room falls silent as they sense a change in the air and mum looks at me with a worried expression and whispers, "What?"

Shaking my head, I take Oliver's hand and look at Florence, David and finally my mum. Smiling, I give Oliver's hand a squeeze and say gently, "Do you remember when we went Christmas shopping and met Nancy?"

Mum nods but looks baffled. "Of course." "Do you remember that she mentioned Sadie Carmichael then and told us about the pregnancy test?"

I watch the penny drop in my mum's eyes as all the fight goes out of her and the tears fall. "Please don't tell me what I think you're about to say."

Nodding, I say with a slight break to my voice, "Yes, mum. You asked me why I believed Oliver and turned a blind eye to his faults. Well, I did so because he is the father of my baby."

For a moment, everyone stands as if frozen in time. Normal life carries on all around us but our lives will never be the same again. I have just thrown a devastating grenade into the room that will blow this family apart.

Then comes the storm.

Mum's scream fills the room as she cries, "You stupid girl, I won't allow it."

Florence makes to speak and mum says angrily, "Shut the fuck up all of you. No, I will not allow Lily to bring a child of *his* into the world, I would rather die first."

She looks so angry I start to shake as she advances towards me. "I gave you everything. Everything, you hear me. I sacrificed my entire life for you and this is how you repay me. Well no, it's not ok and you will have that *creature* terminated."

The pain hits me in the deepest part of my soul as my mother reveals herself to me for the first time. Gone is the caring mother who I ran to with all my problems. Gone is the woman whose opinion I valued and company I enjoyed. In her place is a stranger and a mad one at that because she is mad; I can see it in her eyes as she snarls, "You're just like him. Peter thought he could do what he wanted and you're no different. Well, let me tell you this, he didn't get away with it and neither will you."

She paces the room and I see the worry on the faces all around me as my mother unravels before their eyes. "What do you mean, he didn't get away with it?"

My voice comes out in a frightened whisper and she laughs bitterly. "He cheated on me the whole time we were married. He didn't care for my feelings and the whole hospital knew. I was a laughingstock and all because of *him*. Then he met

Melissa. That tart fresh out of nursing college and he dared to tell me he was leaving me for her. Yes, her - almost a child and every bit as stupid. We were going to be pushed aside for a younger model and I wasn't having it."

I start to shake as I fear the words I know are coming. "What did you do?"

Laughing, she looks like a maniac as she is transported back in time and her face contorts with a twisted rage. "The stupid man had a heart attack, probably because of her demands. Well, unfortunately, he pulled through and when I went to visit him it was to plead with him to stay. But that bastard had no intention of staying and facing his responsibilities, so when he slept, I made sure he never woke up."

I scream, at least I think it's me because I can't hear anything else. All around me are the screams of pain as my whole life comes crashing down around me. Mum starts laughing, and it's the sound of madness. The tears won't stop falling as I face the truth of my past.

My mother murdered my father.

Suddenly, all hell breaks loose as she totally loses control and grabs the bottle of gin, still lying where it fell at David's feet. She smashes it on the edge of the fireplace and holds the shards of glass in front of her and cries, "I would rather kill you than let you suffer at the hands of this rapist's spawn. I will kill you all rather than let my child be a part of this tragic excuse for a family."

She turns to me and says in a calm, almost sweet voice, "Get your things, darling, Christmas is over and we must go home. Thank Florence and David for a lovely time but it's time to go."

I can see Florence shaking, with tears running down her face, as mum stands by the doorway brandishing the broken bottle in front of her. We are all trapped in this room and I see the stricken look in David's eye as the scent of gin dominates our senses. Oliver pulls me behind him and mum screams, "Now, Lily, don't make me punish you. You're not too old to go on the naughty step, young lady."

She turns to Florence. "Honestly, these children are so disrespectful these days. I can only apologise for my daughter's behaviour. Just wait until her father gets home, he'll discipline her."

I think we all feel the fear as she starts to hum to herself and I see Toby turn and tap something on his phone. Mum can't see because she is smiling and says brightly, "You do have such a lovely home, Florence. You really must give me some tips. You know, Peter and I discussed moving to a new home just last week. Maybe we will be neighbours, that would be such fun, wouldn't it?"

She stares at me from across the room and says irritably, "Don't dawdle, Lily, it's time to go home. If you're good, I'll read you a bedtime story but only if you come with me now."

I'm not sure what to do and whisper, "I'm coming, mummy."

Oliver pulls me back, saying urgently, "No."

Mum's head snaps around and she shouts, "Is that boy bothering you, Lily?"

"No! No, of course not. He was just telling me to do what you said."

She nods with approval. "Yes, such a good boy. Maybe he would like to come over for tea sometimes. Would you like that, darling, a playdate at the weekend?"

I nod and try to sound as normal as possible. "Um… yes, that would be good."

I see the blue lights flashing from the street as I look past my mother. Toby nods and I realise what he was doing behind his back. The only way I can think of keeping everyone safe is to say quickly, "I think our taxis arrived, mum."

She beams around the room. "Lovely, well, thank you again, Florence, David. You have two lovely boys you must be so proud. We had a lovely Christmas, didn't we darling?"

I nod sadly, "Yes, mummy."

She looks at her watch and smiles. "Goodness, your father's shift will be over soon, we had better get back. Such a shame that the medical staff have to work on Christmas day. Oh well, you can't stop being sick just because it's Christmas, can you Florence?"

She grins and then holds out her hand. "Come, darling, let's go home."

34

I walk with my mother's hand in mine just like we used to. I feel the soft hands of a capable woman who made everything better. I walk with the past and remember happier times and I walk into the future on my own because as we reach the police car, I say quickly, "Here we are, mum, a nice warm taxi to take us home."

My heart twists with fear, as she raises the broken bottle and waves it madly in the air. "Goodness, what a lovely taxi. Such interesting insignia, what did you say the company was called?"

She peers at the lettering on the car and I interrupt, "Quickly mum, in you get, the meter's running."

The police officer looks at her and smiles, saying calmly, "Good evening, Mrs Adams, have you had a nice Christmas?"

"Lovely, thank you, my dear. What a shame that you have to work."

He nods and says breezily, "Somebody has to. Anyway, let me take your luggage and put it in the back safely."

I hold my breath, as he reaches over and gently grasps the bottle and she looks at him in surprise. "Goodness, I forgot I had that. Thank you."

The relief is overwhelming as he disarms my mother and helps her into the back of the police car. She looks up and says sternly, "Come on, Lily, don't dawdle."

Fighting back the tears, I say softly, "I'll be along in a minute, mum, I forgot my rabbit."

She laughs and the last thing I hear her saying before they close the door on her is, "Children, where would they be without their mothers?"

As the door slams and pulls away from the curb, I picture her alone in the back of the car. What will she think when she reaches the station and how will they deal with her? As the taillights disappear around the corner, I break down in the street. My knees give way and it's only when two strong arms lift me before I hit the snowy ground, that I realise I'm not alone. As Oliver's family crowd around me and add their embrace to his, I know that I am now where I belong.

We must stand outside for a good five minutes before Florence says gently, "Come inside, it's been quite a day, let's go where we can talk in the warm."

As Christmas day turns to night, we have much to talk about. There is no television and no loud party games. Just the urgent conversation of a group of people who have had their world turned upside down. It's a time to heal and make sense of a past that none of us knew we had. It's a time for discussion, not recriminations and adjustment.

By the time the clock announces it's now Boxing day, we fall into our respective beds, exhausted and changed forever. There is one bed that remains empty and I try not to think of my mother alone and frightened in an unfamiliar place. Florence called the station and was told that mum had been taken straight to a psychiatric hospital and she thinks she's in a lovely hotel. I'm glad of that at least because she's still my mum and I care what happens to her. I just hope she gets the help she so badly needs and maybe one day we can build a new relationship. Time will need to be a great healer in our case because there is so much to forgive. But she is still my mum and nothing will ever change that. I know she loved me but I just didn't know how much.

35

"Hurry up, Oliver, we can't be late."

"We wouldn't be if you didn't insist on bringing everything but the kitchen sink."

Turning around, I laugh as I see him hauling a sack full of Christmas presents into the back of the car and then my gaze falls to my pride and joy, Alyssia.

I still can't believe that we actually did it. The little bundle of hope and innocence that gurgles in her car seat is the sunshine of all our lives and we couldn't be happier.

Oliver jumps into the driver's seat and groans. "There - finally. You didn't have to go overboard you know."

"Maybe not but I thought I should pull out all the stops this year due to the fact that last year was destroyed."

Oliver looks at me with concern and I smile softly. "Let's hope this year passes without a hitch."

"Well, it couldn't be worse than last year. I'm just surprised we're celebrating at all. It will always be a reminder of what happened and I'll never celebrate Christmas without thinking of how our lives were nearly destroyed that day."

I fall silent as he starts the engine and feel a little nervous myself about the days ahead. This year, compared to last, is completely different because we have all had some major adjustments to make. Reaching out, I squeeze Oliver's hand and he smiles. "We made it though, didn't we Lily flower?"

"Yes, we did, which shows our strength."

We settle down for the journey and I think of the dark days that followed the devastating revelations on Christmas day. Oliver has done incredibly well, in fact, we all have, due to the counselling we received in the months afterwards. Even now, we are still learning to deal with what happened and I couldn't be prouder of Oliver as he came to terms with who he really is. It was difficult, to put it mildly, but he talked it through and with professional help and the love of his family, me included, he is doing well.

Alyssia is sleeping peacefully and my heart swells with love for her. There was never any question that we would keep the baby. Both Oliver and I never gave it a second thought and although we are still engaged, we were in no hurry to marry. We both graduated and Oliver took a position with a bank in the city. The salary is good and has enabled us to buy our own home on the outskirts, near to his parents and I have put my career on hold to bring up our daughter.

Life is good just one year on and I can't believe how far we've all come.

"How was your mother when you visited?"

Oliver's question brings me back to the present and I sigh. "Much the same. She still thinks she's staying in a five-star hotel and that my father is working. The doctors have said that she's retreated to a place in her mind where she feels comfortable, probably because she can't deal with the reality of what happened."

"Do you think she'll ever understand what she did?"

"In a way, I hope not because at the moment she's happy. If she understood the horror of what happened, it may destroy her all over again."

I sigh. "You know, Oliver, I will never forgive her but she's still my mother. I suppose it just makes me more determined to be the best one I can for Alyssia. I want her to feel loved and have a happy childhood with no secrets. I don't want her to feel scared when I'm in the room and want her to grow up with two parents who love her."

He smiles and I recognise the look. Oliver dotes on his daughter. Gone is the cheeky player who was the subject of every girl's fantasy and in its place is a doting father and fiancé who couldn't treat his family any better than he does. I love him so much and am glad we are taking things one step at a time. He needs to heal and adjust to his situation as do I and there will be plenty of time for marriage and more babies when we have come to terms with who we both are.

It doesn't take long before he pulls the car on the driveway and I look at the house that has become so familiar to me.

The door swings open almost immediately and Florence rushes out, looking so excited we both laugh. "Well, someone's happy."

Oliver laughs as she goes straight to the passenger door and wrenches it open, cooing, "She's here, come to nanny, darling, oh look at how perfect she is. She really is the most beautiful baby in the world."

"Um... hi, mum."

Oliver grins and Florence laughs. "Sorry, darling, but you can't blame me."

He laughs. "It's fine, we kind of understand, after all, she is our baby."

We leave Florence to take Alyssia inside and I help Oliver unload the luggage.

David rushes out to help and I watch with tears in my eyes as he hugs Oliver and says happily, "Good to see you, son."

Oliver looks just as happy and I think about how far they have all come.

He turns to me and holds out his arms and I walk into them happily. He hugs me hard and whispers, "Good to see you, darling."

As I snuggle into David's arms, my heart lifts because David has turned out to be fantastic. He really stepped up and took charge after what happened and became the rock this family, in fact, all of us, so badly needed at our darkest time. He became like a father to me and helped me just as much as his own family. In fact, they have both been amazing and although it turned their world upside down; they remained standing and helped us all through a desperate time.

We head inside and I smile at the magical atmosphere that Florence has created. As usual, she has left nothing to chance and all around me the magic of Christmas sparkles inside every fairy light and in the flame of every candle dancing in the light. The scent of cinnamon mixed with orange lifts my heart and I smile as I see the colourful mocktails lined up on a silver tray on the island unit in the kitchen. As I spy the rather large pile of gifts under the tree, David laughs. "She's gone a little overboard this year, I can only apologise in advance."

Oliver groans. "No prizes for guessing who most of them are for. Our house isn't that big, dad, where does she think we will put them all?"

Florence wanders in holding Alyssia against her chest and looks so happy it brings a smile to all our faces. "Don't judge me, Oliver, because I won't apologise for spoiling my granddaughter."

She looks across at me and smiles warmly. "Happy Christmas, Lily darling. How's your mother?"

My heart swells with love for the woman who has become like a mother to me. She always asks after mine and shows a genuine concern for her well-being. Far from hating her for what she did, she has tried to understand and I know she herself has faced the most difficult year of her life coming to terms with the fact that her own baby died all those years ago and Oliver isn't who they both thought he was.

A lump forms in my throat as Oliver puts his arm around her and says happily, "Thanks, mum."

The brightness in her eyes shows how much his words mean to her because I know she's worried about him. The days and weeks following the revelation were hard on them all. Oliver struggled to come to terms with who he is and they battled to understand what happened all those years ago.

"Is anybody home?"

Florence smiles happily and yells, "In here, darling."

We look up as Toby enters the room beaming, with his arm draped across the shoulders of his girlfriend of the past three months.

She smiles nervously, and it reminds me of when I stood there one year ago to the day. This is their first Christmas together and I am curious to learn more about the woman who appears to have made Toby grow up almost overnight.

She catches my eye and I smile warmly and I can tell she's grateful. She looks nervous, so I head over and kiss her on the cheek. "I'm Lily, Oliver's girlfriend. I'm pleased to meet you."

She smiles shyly as Florence moves across and hands me Alyssia before pulling Jenny into her arms. "Welcome, darling, it's good to see you."

She pulls away and introduces the others before pulling Jenny off to show her the pretty room she has prepared for her. Watching them, Toby laughs. "That should keep mum occupied for an hour or so." He turns to Oliver and grins. "Good to see you, bro."

I have to turn away as they hug it out because it always makes me come undone as I see the difference in them just one year on. Most surprising of all is the relationship that Toby and Oliver have built after the devastating revelations. If anything, it brought them closer together because Toby fully understood how Oliver must now be feeling. He always felt like the outsider but, as it turns out, that was Oliver. They have reached an understanding and although still have their moments, have formed a deeper relationship in the face of adversity.

David hands them both a non-alcoholic beer and turns to me. "Mocktail, Lily?"

Grinning, I accept the colourful drink and raise my glass in a toast. "To new beginnings and a much better Christmas than the last."

Toby groans. "I'll drink to that."

David nods. "Me too. It can't get any worse, surely?"

Oliver laughs. "No, only good things for this family from now on."

As we sip our drinks, the fire dances in the grate and the sound of Christmas carols reinforce the magic of the season. As I stare around at my new family with my pride and joy in my arms, I say a silent prayer for my own father and mother. They may not be here to enjoy this with me but there will always be a part of them I carry with me wherever I go. I can't dwell on the past because it would destroy my future. I have to let that go to move on and as Oliver moves across and pulls me and Alyssia into his arms; I have everything I need right here in this room. A family of my own and one that I will never give up trying to make happy.

36

As soon as I leave Jenny to unpack, I head back to see the rest of my family. However, before I even reach the top of the stairs, I see David walking towards me and I smile. "Hey, are you ok?"

Nodding, I settle into his arms as he kisses the top of my head and says softly, "Come with me."

He leads me into our room and sits on the bed, patting the space beside him. "David, we have guests."

Laughing, he shakes his head. "It's ok, I'm not going to pounce on you, no matter how much I'm loving that thought."

Rolling my eyes, I sit beside him and say a little anxiously, "Is everything ok?"

"Couldn't be better." He smiles sweetly. "I just wanted to check you were ok. I know you were worried how they would react coming here today and I think you can relax because they all seem fine."

"Yes, I can see that. You know, all I want is for this Christmas to go without a hitch. After last year, I just want closure on the whole experience. Now we have Alyssia and Toby appears happy with

238

Jenny, I just want us to be a normal family with no dramas."

He nods in agreement. "Same. Anyway, I just wanted to check on you."

He stands and grins. "Well, I had better get back. I haven't had a cuddle with my granddaughter yet and once you get downstairs, I'll have no chance."

He winks and heads to the door and as he leaves; I think of how far we've all come.

It's not been easy, but we got there in the end – at least I think we did. It was so hard dealing with everything Alice threw at us in one cluster filled, time bomb. The most devastating – for me anyway – was the knowledge that Oliver wasn't the baby I gave birth to. Finding out that my baby had died in childbirth was very hard to come to terms with.

Then there was the realisation of where Oliver came from. He has struggled with that one and who can blame him? However, I know my son and he is just that - *my son*. I may not be his mother by blood but I am in every other way. I couldn't love him more if he were my own child and actually it made no difference at all to my feelings for him. He became my number one priority and with David's help we guided him through the shadows and into the light.

Then there was Toby. Finding out the truth that David was his natural father was bittersweet for him. I never realised he harboured so much resentment for something that just wasn't true. He has also found it difficult to come to terms with what he learned and has gradually shaken off the past and can now look forward to the future. The fact he has formed a new bond with Oliver makes me so happy. Yes, despite everything those boys will pull through. We all will.

As I head off to join the celebrations, I think of Lily. Of all of us she concerned me the most because where we had each other, she had nobody. I insisted that she move in with us because I couldn't bear to think of her alone in that flat she shared with her mother when she wasn't at Uni. I also paid for counselling for her because finding out that your mother murdered your father was a shock that could have pulled her under. The pregnancy turned out to be a godsend because it helped us all look to the future with something positive to focus on. At first, I worried they were too young to shoulder the responsibility. The state of their fragile minds also concerned me and that is why I wanted to keep them all close. I helped Lily and Oliver through the whole thing and looked after Alyssia as much as possible to help ease the shock that a new baby brings.

Then there is Alice. I don't think I'll ever forget watching a woman descend into madness as rapidly as she did that day. Thinking of what she lived with for all those years makes my blood run cold. If anything, I'm glad she came last Christmas because it meant the truth came out, despite how devastating that was. Just imagining her caring for Alyssia makes my blood run cold. At least she's now getting the help she needs, and it's doubtful she'll be released for a very long time. Lily still visits her once a month and I know it's hard for her. However, she still loves her mother but I know there is a part of that love that died that day.

When she told us she would be a 'stay at home mum' I worried if that was the right thing to do. After all, I was more than willing to step up and be their childminder and would have loved every minute of it. However, I also recognise that Lily is determined to be a good mum to Alyssia and who can argue with that? They are a tight little family unit and it's good to see.

I see Toby heading my way and smile. "I've left Jenny unpacking."

"Yes, I thought as much. I'm just going to check she's ok."

"She seems lovely, Toby. Don't mess this one up." I wink to take the sting from my words and he grins. "Don't worry, I'm not about to. You know, Jenny is the first girl I can actually see a future with."

I laugh. "After three months?"

"Yes." He looks thoughtful. "I never really understood what makes a person want to be with someone for longer. Most of my other girlfriends bored me rigid after a few weeks but Jenny's different." His face softens and I smile to myself. "You see, mum, she's sweet and kind but with an edge to her, that takes no shit. She challenges me mentally because she's as sharp as a razor. I think she's a beautiful person inside and out and when she's not around, it's as if something is missing. Is that normal?"

Reaching out, I draw him in for a hug and say happily, "It sounds as if you're in love, Toby. Goodness, who'd have thought?"

I tease him but his words fill me with a happiness that means so much. Seeing my boys happy is all I want. Knowing Toby has found someone like Jenny is the best present a mother can get and as he pulls back, he kisses me softly on the cheek. "Thanks, mum. I love you."

He walks away leaving me in shock and the tears spill down my cheeks which I am reluctant to wipe away. Toby said he loves me. I don't think I have ever heard him say those words to me and I lean against the wall for support. Three little words that hold so much meaning. At this moment everything comes good. We made it; *I* made it and now I know the shadows have finally gone and we can be a proper family.

"Are you ok, Florence?"
I see Lily looking at me anxiously as she cradles Alyssia in her arms. Brushing away my tears, I smile and hold out my arms for my grandchild. "Just feeling a little sentimental. Don't mind me, I'll shake it off in a minute."

Lily smiles. "Well, Christmas is a sentimental time of the year."

I see the pain in her eyes and know she is remembering this time last year and I say with concern, "More importantly, are you ok, Lily?"

"To be honest, I couldn't be better, does that make me a bad person?"

"Why would it?"

"Because of mum. She will never see Alyssia grow up like a normal grandmother. She will never be free like we are and she has lost everything based on what she did all those years ago."

I shake my head sadly as I relish the feeling of holding this precious baby in my arms. I also feel sad for Alice because this is something I would never want to miss out on. "I think your mother is happy in her own way, Lily. She is getting the help she needs and probably doesn't even know what she's missing."

Lily looks worried and says in a small voice. "Do you think I have it in me?"

"Have what?"

"The madness."

I look at her with concern. "Of course not, why do you even think that?"

"Because she's my mother and I'm part of her. What if I have the same capability that she had? Do you think that one day I will fall apart if anything bad happens to me?"

Her words alarm me because that has always been a thought at the back of my mind but I can see how distressed she is and say firmly, "Listen to me. You are your own person and it's up to you to shape your life and now you have the knowledge not to make the mistakes the rest of us did. Look at us all, we're all struggling to overcome some form of weakness inside us. Take David for instance. He has done something that will live with him for the rest of his life and the drinking was a consequence of that. Ultimately, he pulled through and is a stronger person for it; how he has dealt with everything this year proves that. Look at Oliver, and who his father is. Don't you think he worries every day that he has some of his father's characteristics? He knows that he will do anything not to be that person and he won't be. The knowledge has given him the strength to be a better person, and he already is. You see, Lily, knowledge is a powerful weapon and we must be grateful that we have it. It will make us stronger and able to choose a path that steers us away from the mistakes of the past. So, don't think you will even remotely be the same as your mother because you are not her. In fact, it will make you a better one because you won't want your children to feel the same as you did and still do and will do everything you can to prevent that happening."

Lily nods and the emotion in her eyes makes me hold my breath as she leans across and kisses me softly on the cheek. "Thank you, you're a very special person, Florence."

"Not really, darling, but you are kind to say so."

"No, I mean it, you are. Of everyone, you've had the most to deal with but you stood strong while everyone around you crumbled. You held this family together despite the terrible things that happened to you. You could have walked away, but you stayed and fought for your family. I want to be like you, Florence. I want to be that mother and wife that stays at home and cares. The pivot for the family and the centre of it. My mother always looked down on those women that didn't work and stayed at home to care for their families. She would hate that I am now one of them but actually it is her I pity more. I've come to realise that without a strong wife and mother, a family is poorer for it. Of everyone, Florence, you have worked the hardest and given the most value to the job you do. So, thank you because you have shown me what an amazing woman looks like and if I can be even half as amazing as you, I will count myself as being very fortunate."

She smiles at her baby and strokes her hair lovingly before saying softly, "A mother's love is a powerful thing, isn't it? It's unconditional and no matter what she does, I will always be there for her. Nothing will ever break the bond we have and I'll always put her first. Unlike my mother, I will not stifle her and try to protect her from the knocks she'll face in life because ultimately those knocks will shape her into a strong woman. I'm glad we have you to show us how it's done. I'm sorry to be so sentimental but I just wanted you to hear it from me."

As we share a moment so special, it means everything to me. I never had a daughter of my own and I look on Lily as the daughter I never had. I feel emotional as I think about the love I have formed for the brave girl before me. I have grown to love and respect her over the last year and couldn't be happier that she is part of our family.

As we walk back to the others, it's as equals. Two strong women who have learned a valuable lesson. Two strong women who have faced their darkest time and come through and now we have Alyssia to mould and shape into an amazing person who I hope will never have to learn the lessons of her mother and grandmother. If that happens, we can give her the weapons to deal with whatever life throws at her and win.

The End

Thank you for reading The Woman Who Destroyed Christmas. If you have enjoyed the story, I would be so grateful if you could post a review on Amazon. It really helps other readers when deciding what to read and means everything to the Author who wrote it.

READ ON FOR MORE BOOKS BY M J HARDY

HAVE YOU READ?

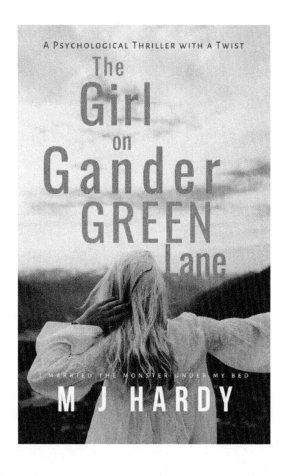

A PSYCHOLOGICAL THRILLER WITH A TWIST

The
Girl
on
Gander
GREEN
Lane

I MARRIED THE MONSTER UNDER MY BED

M J HARDY

A Chilling Psychological Thriller with a Twist.

When a perfect marriage, the perfect husband and perfect life is nothing but an illusion.

Then one night, the nightmare reveals itself.

Sarah Standon is living the dream, at least that's what everyone tells her.
She is the wife of a successful solicitor who looks like a movie star.
They live a Stepford existence and appear to have it all.
But then one fateful night, everything changes.
A terrible accident leaves Sarah alone to deal with a situation so frightening that she starts to question her grip on reality.
Her perfect life has been exposed as the lie it always was and she loses everything.
She thought that was the worst that could happen.
She was wrong.

HAVE YOU READ?

How well do you really know your husband!

When Tom Mahoney was mugged on his way home from work, they thought it was the worst thing that could happen.
They were wrong.
When Tina & Harry found out they couldn't have more children, they thought that was the worst thing that could happen.
They were wrong.
When the new teacher Isabel Rawlins arrives, she brings with her a secret that's about to blow their respectable worlds apart.

Five lives all intertwined and heading on a collision course.
Will their relationships survive, or is one or more couple about to find out there's a husband thief in their midst?

Remember, if you have trust, you can conquer anything. When trust goes, madness sets in.
This tale comes with a twist it's doubtful you will see coming.

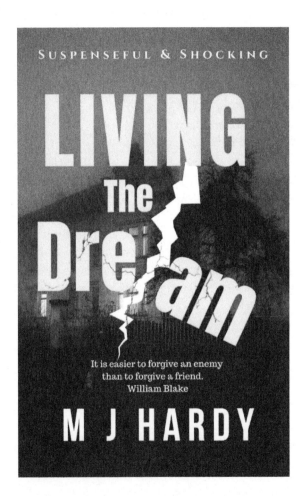

SUSPENSEFUL & SHOCKING

LIVING The Dream

It is easier to forgive an enemy
than to forgive a friend.
William Blake

M J HARDY

Have you ever wondered what it's like to have it all?

Four couples live a charmed life behind the security gates of an exclusive development. To everyone else, they have a dream life. Beautiful homes, designer clothes and more money than sense.

Behind closed doors, the story is very different. Beauty is skin deep and when you scratch the surface the blood runs cold. Betrayal, dishonesty and lies are about to blow their worlds apart and not everyone will survive.

Who is telling the truth and who is hiding a secret they would do anything to protect?

Money doesn't buy happiness; it buys a more expensive kind of trouble.

When your friends are your enemies in disguise, expect things to get ugly.

Printed by Amazon Italia Logistica S.r.l.
Torrazza Piemonte (TO), Italy

10621587R00151